Giovanni Battista
PERGOLESI
1710—1736

D1526598

First page, *Sinfonia to an Unknown Opera*. Stockholm: Kungl. Musikaliska Akademien. No. 35.

Giovanni Battista
PERGOLESI
1710–1736

A Thematic Catalogue of the Opera Omnia
with an Appendix listing omitted compositions

by MARVIN E. PAYMER

PENDRAGON PRESS   NEW YORK, NEW YORK

From the Same Publisher

SERIES I   RILM Retrospectives

A series of annotated bibliographies sponsored by RILM
(International Repertory of Music Literature)

SERIES II   THEMATIC CATALOGUES

Library of Congress Cataloging in Publication Data

Paymer, Marvin E
    Giovanni Battista Pergolesi, 1710-1736.

    Bibliography: p.
    Includes index.
    1. Pergolesi, Giovanni Battista, 1710-1736--Thematic
catalogs. I. Title.
ML134.P613A35   016.78'092'4   77-1419
ISBN 0-918728-01-0

To the Memory of

MICHAEL PAYMER   1883-1966

CONTENTS

ILLUSTRATIONS

PREFACE

This catalogue is intended to facilitate the location and identification of the music published in Giovanni Battista Pergolesi Opera Omnia,[1] with an indication of doubtful and spurious works as reported in the literature, and an appendix listing works attributed to Pergolesi but omitted from the Opera Omnia. On the basis of available information, it appears that of the 148 works in the complete works edition, 69 are misattributed, 49 are of questionable parentage, and only 30 may be considered genuine. In other words, as much as 80% of the Opera Omnia may not be by Pergolesi.

Clearly, few composers are more in need of a thematic catalogue than Pergolesi. Few have more "spuriosities" to their credit. The present catalogue is a necessary first step that will help, one hopes, in the identification of Pergolesiana, true and false. However, full authentication of Pergolesi's output -- to the extent that this may be possible -- must await considerable further research.[2]

The Opera Omnia is noteworthy not only for its high percentage of misattributions, but also for its errors of omission. The "Appendix," compiled from library holdings and catalogues, and from lists appearing in various monographs, biographies and articles, includes a large number of works attributed to Pergolesi which were omitted from the "complete works edition." It must be emphasized that no attempt has been made to verify the information provided in the references; a study of the sources does not lie within the scope of this catalogue.

---

[1]Filippo Cafarelli, ed., Giovanni Battista Pergolesi Opera Omnia, 26 vols. (Rome: Gli Amici della Musica da Camera, 1941).

[2]Toward this end, the author has for some time been examining the question of authenticity of the instrumental works attributed to Pergolesi, including many which do not appear in the Opera Omnia.

The "Thematic Catalogue" presents the musical incipits of the works in the Opera Omnia, transcribed into the Simplified Plaine and Easie Code.[3]

The "Thematic Locator" is an index of the 659 musical incipits in the Opera Omnia, transposed to C major and C minor by applying a computer program to the coded and key-punched themes. The transposed incipits have then been alphabetized using another computer program. A fringe benefit of the locator became apparent in the discovery of duplicate appearances of a number of entries.

The "Index to the Thematic Catalogue" lists composers, titles and first lines of works in the Opera Omnia in the conventional manner. However, it should be pointed out that the terms "Sonata," "Sinfonia," "Concertino," and "Concerto" are more or less interchangeable in this catalogue, as they are in the edition. A second index pertains to the Appendix, listing attributed works omitted from the Opera Omnia.

---

[3]Barry S. Brook, "The Simplified Plaine and Easie Code System for Notating Music: a Proposal for International Adoption," Fontes Artis Musicae, XII/2-3 (1965), 156-160; see summary below.

The Simplified Plaine and Easie Code

This code system, developed by Barry S. Brook, is a computer-oriented method of notating music by numbers, letters, and other typewriter symbols.[4] Tempo, key signature, and meter in that order are given first in parentheses. The symbol # indicates a sharp and the symbol b a flat; thus a coded key signature within the parentheses of #FC means the key of D major, while one of bBEA means the key of Eb major. When the key is the relative minor, the coded key signature is followed by the word "minor"; thus a coded key signature of #F minor means the key of E minor. A triple blank space, separated by commas, means there are no sharps or flats in the key signature. An exclamation mark means that the composer's key signature is "incorrect," a common Baroque occurrence; thus bBEA ! means that despite only three flats, the actual key of the incipit is Ab major.

Duration:

Given in numbers -- 1 2 3 4 5 6 7 8 9 0 -- for both notes and rests. The numbers precede pitch letters and remain in effect, crossing bar lines, until a different duration number appears.

1 whole note or rest	3 thirty-second note or rest
2 half note or rest	5 sixty-fourth note or rest
4 quarter note or rest	7 hundred-twenty-eighth note or rest
8 eighth note or rest	9 breve
6 sixteenth note or rest	0 longa

Dotted notes indicated by period: 2. C = dotted half-note C.

Rests indicated by a hyphen: 4C-2-=

Ties by underscore: 2C_4C =

---

[4]See footnote 3. A summary of the Simplified Plaine and Easie Code (on which this description is based) has been published in Barry S. Brook, Thematic Catalogues in Music (Hillsdale, N. Y.: Pendragon Press, 1972), p. 43.

Triplets and other unusual rhythmic groupings are enclosed in parentheses preceded by duration number:

8(CDE) =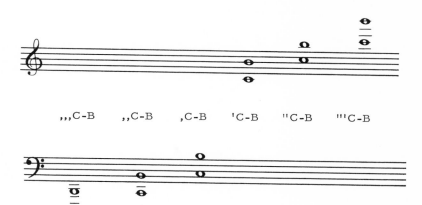

Fermata indicated by parentheses around a single pitch or rest: (C)

Pitch:

Given in letters: A B C D E F G

Accidentals immediately precede pitch letters as in conventioned notation: Sharp = #. Flat = b. Natural = n. Double sharp = x. Double flat = bb.

Register (Octave Placement) indicated by commas or apostrophes placed in front of duration and pitch symbols and remaining in effect until a different register sign appears:

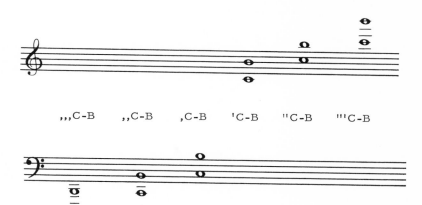

,,,C-B   ,,C-B   ,C-B   'C-B   "C-B   '''C-B

Additional Symbols:

/	Bar line	//	Double bar line	t	Trill
g	Grace note	/-/	Full measure rest	F-4	Bass clef
://	Repeat	/-3/	Three measure rest		

The symbols used in the Simplified Plaine and Easie Code are mnemonic whenever possible. A good idea of how the code works can be gleaned from the examples given below in which the code symbols appear directly beneath the musical symbols to which they refer:

Item 7.

(Allegro, #F, C) '4G B "D G / 3F E 8.D _ 2D

Item 49a.

(Andante, #FC, C) 2- "nC _ / 4C C (C) 8- E / gE 4.D

Item 49b.

(Allegro moderato, #FC, 2/4) "8D 6D D F F D D / 8E 'A

Using the Catalogue

The systematic arrangement of this catalogue has been based upon the division of the music appearing in the Opera Omnia into three categories: instrumental, sacred vocal, and secular vocal. Each of these in turn has been divided into sub-categories by genre in which the authentic works, if any, are listed first, followed by the doubtful (?) and then the misattributed (X) works. For doubtful and misattributed works, page references to evidence in monographs and articles cited in the bibliography are given.

A typical entry provides the following information:

FIRST LINE,   a) catalogue number (one for each entire work) and, where applicable:

                           b) ? (doubtful) or X (spurious)

                           c) name of probable composer

                           d) number/page of reference(s) cited (see bibliography)

SECOND LINE,   e) conventional title (in capital letters)

                           f) VOLUME:page in the Opera Omnia (if there is a second reference cited, the VOLUME:page in the Opera Omnia appears on the third line)

THIRD LINE,   g) musical incipit.

SAMPLE ENTRY:

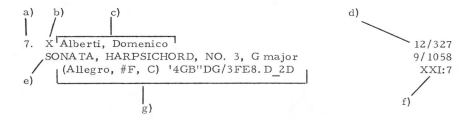

For a composition in several sections, letters are added to the catalogue number to designate each section. For example, the four movements
of a suite would be designated 3. a b c d (see page 1, catalogue number 3), or
the thirty numbers of an opera would be designated 146. a b c . . . dd (see
page 40, catalogue number 146). In such cases, the first line of each sec-
tional entry includes the catalogue letter, the title of the movement or textual incipit (in lower case letters), an indication of solos and ensembles in
parentheses, and the page in the Opera Omnia, while the second line contains
the musical incipit. The voices necessary for performances are symbolized
by the following abbreviations:

S solo   = solo soprano
A solo   = solo alto
T solo   = solo tenor
Bar solo = solo baritone
B solo   = solo bass

Appropriate combinations of these abbreviations are used to indicate duets,
trios, quartets and quintets.

SAMPLE ENTRY:

49. X   9/1057
       MASS, SATB & ORCHESTRA, D major   8/410
                                                              XXIII: 64
    a. Kyrie
       (Andante, #FC, C) 2-"nC_/4CC(C)8-E/gE4. D8GgG4. F
    b. Gloria in excelsis Deo   75
       (Allegro moderato, #FC, 2/4) "8D6DDFFDD/8E'A
    c. Laudamus te (S solo)   78
       (Andantino, #FCG, 3/4) '8. A"6E4ED/DC-/

       etc.

In untitled movements, as for example in those of the trio sonatas (see page 3, catalogue number 12), all information is included on one line. In the rare cases where individual sections of a work have different attributions, a line is added above the first indicating where applicable, ? (doubtful) or X (spurious), and the name of the probable composer.

SAMPLE ENTRY:

147. X Galuppi, Baldassare and Chiarini, Pietro   18/312
     IL GELOSO SCHERNITO   13/540
                                                          III:5

  a. X Galuppi, Baldassare   12/321
     Sinfonia   18/315
     (Allegro vivo, #F, C) "8G-gA6GFGA8GD'BG/

    ACT I:
  b. X Chiarini, Pietro   10
     Son moglie, non schiava
     (Allegretto,   , 3/8) '8G/"6C'G8. G6F/6. E3F8G

  etc.

Acknowledgements

I am particularly indebted to Professor Barry S. Brook, Executive Officer of the Ph.D. Program in Music, Graduate School and Center, The City University of New York, for his constant encouragement and constructive criticism and to Professor Walter Gerboth, Deputy Chairman, Graduate Studies in Music, Brooklyn College, The City University of New York for his very generous help and numerous valuable suggestions. Acknowledgement is also made to Dr. George Logemann and Mr. Gary Berlind, formerly of the New York University Computer Center, who devised the computer transposition program used to prepare the locator index. Special thanks go to Mrs. Joy Berman, formerly of the Computer Center at Queens College, The City University of New York, who revised this program for our purposes, and to Professors Lilia Subrizi and Edvige Agostinelli Coleman for assistance in reading proof. Finally, I must gratefully acknowledge the encouragement and perseverance of my wife, Edye, without whose confidence this catalogue would never have materialized.

Systematic Table of Contents to the Opera Omnia

Diagrammatic Entry

See page no. 1: catalogue no. 1

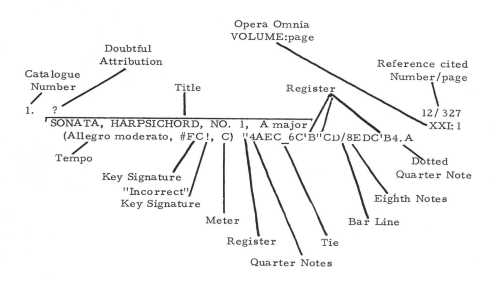

Opera Omnia
VOLUME:page

Reference cited
Number/page

Doubtful
Attribution

Catalogue
Number

Title

Register

1. ?

12/ 327
XXI: 1

SONATA, HARPSICHORD, NO. 1, A major
(Allegro moderato, #FC!, C) ''4AEC_6C'B''CD/8EDC'B4.A

Tempo

Dotted
Quarter Note

Key Signature

"Incorrect"/
Key Signature

Eighth Notes

Meter

Bar Line

Register

Tie

Quarter Notes

Allegro moderato

THEMATIC
CATALOGUE

Title page, *Eight Lessons for the Harpsichord*. London: British Museum. Nos. 206-212.

First page, *Sonata, Harpsichord, no. 1*. London: British Museum. No. 206.

INSTRUMENTAL MUSIC
For Solo Instrument

AUTHENTIC WORKS: None

DOUBTFUL WORKS:

First page, *Sonata, Violin, and Bass*. Cambridge: King's College. No. 231.

Beginning, Second Movement, *Sonata, Violin and Bass*. Cambridge: King's College. No. 231. Also see No. 1.

5.   ?   12/328
      SUITE, HARPSICHORD, NO. 3, D major   XXI:31

  a. Allemande
      (Larghetto, #FC, C) '8F/4F8G3AGFG4A6-AFD/
  b. Minuet   33
      (Moderato, #FC, 3/4) 2.-/8-"D8.C'6B8.A6G/FE8D
  c. Gavotte with Variations   35
      (Allegro moderato, #FC, C) "4D6EDCD4AC/2C

SPURIOUS WORKS:

6.   X   12/327
      SONATA, HARPSICHORD, NO. 2, C major   XXI:3
      (Allegretto, , 3/8) '8G/"E6(CDE)gE6(DC'B)/

7.   X Alberti, Domenico   12/327
      SONATA, HARPSICHORD, NO. 3, G major   9/1058
      (Allegro, #F, C) '4GB"DG/3FE8.D_2D   XXI:7

8.   X   12/327
      SONATA, HARPSICHORD, NO. 4, G major   XXI:11
      (Allegro, #F, 3/8) 6-'GB"D/t8.G3F6G

9.   X   12/327
      SONATA, HARPSICHORD, NO. 5, C major   XXI:14
      (Andantino, , 3/4) '4G/"2C8'(B"CD)/2C

10.   X   12/327
      SONATA, HARPSICHORD, NO. 6, B flat major   XXI:16
      (Andante, bBE, C) '4B"Dt4.F6GA/8B'B

For Two to Four Instruments

AUTHENTIC WORKS: None

DOUBTFUL AND SPURIOUS WORKS:

11.   ?   12/324
      SONATA, CELLO AND CONTINUO, F major   XXI:46
  a. F-4 clef (Comodo, bB, C) '8C/FC-,6(C,BA)(AGF)'D,nB'8C

Title page, *Sonata, Two Violins and Bass*. Uppsala: Universitetsbiblioteket. No. 230.

First page, *Sonata, Two Violins and Bass*. Uppsala: Universitetsbiblioteket. No. 230.

b.   F-4 clef (Allegro, bB, 3/4) 6-'C/4F4.A8G/FE4.F
c.   F-4 clef (Adagio, bB minor, C) '8D4D6(FED)g#G8A4A
d.   F-4 clef (Presto, bB, 2/4) '4FC/,3AG8.F

SONATA I

First page, *Sonata, Two Violins and Continuo* (Domenico Gallo). Washington: Library of Congress. No. 12.

19. X Gallo, Domenico (?)   12/325
     SONATA, 2 VIOLINS AND CONTINUO, NO. 8, E flat major   18/298

   a. (Allegro non troppo, bBEA, 2/4) '8B/"E'B"G6AG/8F'B   V:72
   b. (Andantino, bBE, C) '8B/"t1F_/F_/8F3DEFG6F'B"BbA4G   75
   c. (Allegro, bBEA, 3/4) "4EGE/2.B_/4B2A/2.G/F   78

20. X Gallo, Domenico (?)   12/325
     SONATA, 2 VIOLINS AND CONTINUO, NO. 9, A major   18/298

   a. (Presto, #FCG, ¢) 4-'A"C'A/"E'E"ED/C'A   V:81
   b. (Larghetto, #FC, C) '8A/"4D_6D'A"DF8FE_   86
   c. (Allegro, #FCG, 3/8) '8A"CE/4.E_/8E4D/8CEA/4.A/8A   88

21. X Gallo, Domenico (?)   12/325
     SONATA, 2 VIOLINS AND CONTINUO, NO. 10, F major   18/298

   a. (Moderato, bB, C) 8C/F6AF4.C6DC'8B"B/GC   V:90
   b. (Adagio, bB minor, 3/8) "8A'A"D/8.#C'6A"D'A/   94
   c. (Tempo di minuetto, bB, 3/4) "4FCA/GCB/2A   96

22. X Gallo, Domenico (?)   12/325
     SONATA, 2 VIOLINS AND CONTINUO, NO. 11, D minor   18/298

   a. (Allegro comodo, bB minor, C) "8A/gG4.F6ED2B/   V:99
   b. (Largo, bBE, 3/4) '8F/B"D-F-B/CE-G-C/   102
   c. (Allegro, bB minor, 3/8) "4.A/4D8B/#C4A_/8A4G_/   104

23. X Gallo, Domenico (?)   12/325
     SONATA, 2 VIOLINS AND CONTINUO, NO. 12, E major   18/298

   a. (Allegro, #FCGD, 3/8) "8-EF/4G8A/B'B"B_/B4A_/   V:107
   b. (Adagio, #FCGD, C) "4(F)8-BA4G6BG/8F'B   112
   c. (Presto, #FCGD, 2/4) "4E'6EFGA/8B"C'BA/   113

24. X   12/325
     SONATA, 2 VIOLINS AND CONTINUO, NO. 13, G minor   18/298

   a. (Allegro moderato, bBE minor, C) "2GD/'8B"6C'B8AG   V:117
   b. (Adagio, bBEA, 3/4) "t4EtE'6(BAG)(GFE)/   122
   c. (Allegro, bBE minor, ¢) "1D/E/4D#FG'B/"C'A   125

25. X   12/325
     SONATA, 2 VIOLINS AND CONTINUO, NO. 14, C major   18/298

   a. (Allegro assai,   , C) '2C"C_/4C'B,2G_/G"F_/4FE   V:128
   b. (Largo, bBEAD minor, C) "8C4C8CC4C8C/C4F   133
   c. (Allegro,   , 3/8) "8C'GE/C"6CDEF/8G   135

7

Title page, *Sonata, Two Violins and Continuo* (Domenico Gallo). Stockholm: Kungl. Musikaliska Akademien. No. 12.

First page, *Sonata, Two Violins and Continuo* (Domenico Gallo). Stockholm: Kungl. Musikaliska Akademien. No. 12.

For Five or More Instruments

VI. CONCERTI
ARMONICI

A

Quattro Violini obligati, Alto Viola
Violoncello obligato e Baſſo continuo

Dedicati

All' Illuſtriſſimo Signore
IL SIGNORE CONTE
di BENTINCK

&c.   &c.   &c.

Dal suo humiliſsimo Servitore

C. Ricciotti detto Bacciccia. c. 175---)

LONDON Printed for *John Johnson* at the Harp & Crown in Cheapſide,
of whom may be had,

Title page, *Six Concertini, Four Violins, Viola, Cello, and Continuo*. Washington: Library of Congress. Nos. 26-31.

30.   ? Ricciotti, Carlo (?)   12/322
      CONCERTINO, 4 VIOLINS, VIOLA, CELLO   16/295
      AND CONTINUO, NO. 5, E flat major   VII:67

      a.   (Affettuoso, bBEA, 3/4) "4GFE/DC'B/t8.A6G2A/
      b.   (Presto, bBEA, ¢) "1E/"'C/"2AF/2.B4A/GB   72
      c.   (Largo, bBEA, 3/2) '4-DEFGA/2BE-/   75
      d.   (Vivace, bBEA, 3/4) '8E4GB"8E_/E6DC'B"EDC   77

31.   ? Ricciotti, Carlo (?)   12/322
      CONCERTINO, 4 VIOLINS, VIOLA, CELLO   16/295
      AND CONTINUO, NO. 6, B flat major   VII:83

      a.   (Andante, bBE, C) '8B/"FF6FEDCgC'6tBA8B"B_
      b.   (Presto; a cappella, bBE, 2/2) "1B/G/F/tE/4D'B"DnE/F   87
      c.   (Adagio affettuoso, bBE minor, 12/8) "8D/4G8G8.G6A8B4.D   91
      d.   (Allegro moderato, bBE, 6/8) "8DE/FFFFGA/BBBBGG/   93

32.   ?
      CONCERTO A CINQUE, 3 VIOLINS, VIOLA AND   12/324
      CONTINUO, WITH ACCOMPANIMENT OF   XXI:95
      2 HORNS AND ORGAN, F major

      a.   (Adagio, bB, C) "8C/4.F8G4.G8A/2A-
      b.   (Allegro, bB, C) "6AFAB("'C"BA)(BAG)AFAB   96
      c.   (Grave, bB, C) '4FEF8EC_/CF4A   101
      d.   (Allegro, bB, 2/4) "'4C"B/A-/AG/F   102

33.   ?
      CONCERTO, FLUTE AND STRINGS (2 VIOLINS   12/324
      AND CONTINUO), G major   XXI:71

      a.   (Allegro moderato, #F, C) '4G6B"C8DDDG/6FE4.D
      b.   (Adagio, #F minor, C) "3EF8.G6EGBE3#DE8.F   77
      c.   (Allegro spiritoso, #F, 6/8) "8GD'BGD,B/G   81

34.   ?
      CONCERTO, FLUTE AND STRINGS (2 VIOLINS   12/324
      AND CONTINUO), D major   XXI:86

      a.   (Amoroso, #FC, C) 6-3'(AB"C)/8D6-3(DEF)8E6-3(EFG)
      b.   (Allegro, #FC, C) "4F'6DDDD"4D6DAFE/DC8D_D   90
      c.   (Grave, bB minor, 3/4) "8.A6FgE4D8E/gEt4.#C̄   91
      d.   (Presto, #FC, 3/8) "6.A3G8F'F/FE-/   92

35.   ?
      SINFONIA TO AN UNKNOWN OPERA, G major   12/322
                                                                18/307
      a.   (Allegro, #F, C) '8G6BA8B"DGB"'4D/   XIX:10
      b.   (Andante, bBE minor, 3/4) "8GG_G3B6.A"'3D6.C"3B   12
      c.   (Presto, #F, 3/8) '8G6GBA"C/'B"6DC'BA/8G   13

11

36.   ?   12/324
     SONATA, VIOLIN AND STRINGS (2 VIOLINS, VIOLA,   XXI:54
       AND CONTINUO), B flat major

    a.   (Allegro, bBE, C) "6F/8BGFEDGFE/D
    b.   (Largo, bBE minor, 12/8) "8.D6E8D4G8D8.C6D8C4A8C/   62
    c.   (Allegro, bBE, 3/4) "4B8.-6F8.D'6B/"4GF-/   65

SPURIOUS WORK:

37.   X   12/322
     SINFONIA TO AN UNKNOWN OPERA, D major   18/307
                                                XIX:1
    a.   (Allegro spiritoso, #FC, C) "4F'6AB"CDEFGABGFE/4F
    b.   (Largo, bB minor, 6/8) "8.F6E8D4D'8A/B#C"D   8
    c.   (Tempo di minuetto, #FC, 3/8) "6AG8FE/6DF8E-/   9

SACRED VOCAL MUSIC
Fragments of Masses

DOUBTFUL WORKS:

38. ?
    CREDO, SATB & ORCHESTRA   XIX:supp.
    (Allegro, #FC, C) "4D'A8-"DDD/4CC

39. ?
    AGNUS DEI, SATB & ORCHESTRA (incomplete)   9/1057
    (Largo, #FC minor, C) 4-'8BB4BA/-8BB4BnC/   XXIII:162

SPURIOUS WORKS:

40. X   9/1057
    AGNUS DEI, SSB & ORCHESTRA   XXIII:160
    (Andante,   !, ¢) '2BB/"C'4B"C/2D4DD/

41. X   9/1057
    CREDO, SSAB & ORCHESTRA   XXIII:139
    (Allegro moderato, , C) "2A4BC/C'B"2C

42. X   9/1057
    INCARNATUS, S & ORCHESTRA   XXIII:156
    (Andante sostenuto, #F, C) '4G"3C'6. B"3E6. Dt4. C8C

43. X   9/1057
    SANCTUS, SSB & ORCHESTRA   XXIII:157
    (Larghetto,   minor, C) "4C'B"8CCCC/4C

44. X   9/1057
    SANCTUS, SATB & ORCHESTRA   XXIII:158
    (Lento,   !, C) '2-A_√4AGAB/"C'8BAGAB"C/4D

Masses

AUTHENTIC WORK:

45.   MASS, SSATB & ORCHESTRA, F major   XVIII:2

a. Kyrie eleison
    (Largo, bBE!, C) 2-"4.bD8D/4.C8C4bDC/C
b. Gloria in excelsis Deo   13
    (Allegro spiritoso,   , C) "4.C6ED8CDEF/4.E
c. Laudamus te   27
    (Andante, #F, 3/8) '4.G/"6DE8DC/gC'4.B/
d. Gratias agimus tibi   32
    (Largo,   !, C) '4B8B"4C-/-2C8CC/
e. Domine Deus   37
    (Andante, #FC, C) 2-"6D'A4A8A/6AF4F
f. Qui tollis   43
    (Largo, bBE minor, C) 4."D8GD'B"E/#CD-
g. Quoniam tu solus sanctus   59
    (Andante, bBE, C) '6B"C'4B"8DgD4.C8E/
h. Cum sancto spiritu   63
    (Presto, bB, C) /"C/2CE/4.F6C4C-F/

DOUBTFUL WORKS:

46.   ?   8/410
    MASS, SSATB & ORCHESTRA, D major   XV/2:1

a. Kyrie eleison
    (Grave, #FC, C) 2.-"4D/1D/4C(-)4.F8F/4G
b. Gloria in excelsis Deo   19
    (Allegro, #F, C) '4.B"6C'A"8D4D6EC/'4.B
c. Laudamus te   28
    (Andante, bBE, 3/8) '6.B3F"8DC/gC4D6.E3C/
d. Gratias agimus tibi   32
    (Largo,   , C) "2E4EE/D8DE4#CC/
e. Domine Deus   36
    Alto (Andante molto sostenuto #F minor, 6/8) '4.B/6GF8E
f. Qui tollis   42
    (Largo maestoso, bBEA minor, C) 4.-"8EDD4(-)/4.-8bDCC

g. Quoniam tu solus sanctus   57
    (Allegro,   , C) "2CD/8E6(FED)6. E3C
h. Cum sancto spiritu   61
    (Largo, #FC, C) "2F4ED/2. D4E/1(E)/

47.   ?   9/1057
      MASS, SSATB/SSATB & ORCHESTRA, F major   VI:2

a. Kyrie eleison
    (Maestoso, bB, C) "2. F4F/F-2-/1-/-/-/-/2. E4E/E
b. Gloria in excelsis Deo   27
    (Allegro spiritoso, #FC, C) "4F_6FGFG2A_/8AFDEFFDE/
c. Laudamus te   45
    (Allegretto sostenuto, #FC minor, 6/8) "4. F'B_/6B"GFEDC4B
d. Gratias agimus tibi   48
    (Largo, #F, C) "4D8DD4D#C/2D
e. Domine Deus (A solo)   61
    (Andante molto sostenuto, #F minor, 6/8) 4. -'B/2. B_/2B6AGFE
f. Qui tollis   67
    (Largo, bBE!, C) 2. -4"E/#FG2(-)/2. -4G/nEF
g. Quoniam tu solus sanctus (S solo)   92
    (Andante, #F, C) "8DD_6DGFE/8DD_
h. Cum sancto spiritu   95
    (Largo, bB, C) "1C/C/C/2C4nBB/2C(-)//

SPURIOUS WORKS:

48.   X   9/1057
      MASS, SATB & ORCHESTRA, C major   8/410
                                                            XXIII:1
a. Kyrie eleison
    (Adagio,   , 3/4) "8. C6C4C8C'G/4. A6bB4C
b. Gloria in excelsis Deo   12
    F-4 clef (Con spirito,   , C) ,8C6CC8EG'4C, G/8E, C
c. Laudamus te (S solo)   16
    (Andante sostenuto, #F, 3/8) "8DDD/6(EC'A)8GF/G
d. Gratias agimus tibi   21
    (Allegro,   , C) "8E6CD8E6FD8EC
e. Domine Deus (A solo)   24
    (Comodo, bB, 2/4) '4F8A6GF/"4C'gB"C'4C/
f. Qui tollis   28
    (Andante, bB minor, C) "1D/D/D/4-DDD/1D/2#C-/
g. Quoniam tu solus (B solo)   31
    F-4 clef (Alla breve, #F, C) ,4D8EF4GG/AG2-/
h. Cum sancto spiritu   35
    (Adagio,   , C) "2C'4BB/"CC'2B//'2GA/G
i. Credo   40
    (Allegro,   , C) "8C6CC8CC'B6B"C8D'B/

15

Motets

AUTHENTIC WORKS:

51. DOMINE AD ADIUVANDUM, SSATB & ORCHESTRA   XVII/1:15
     (Allegro assai, #F, C) '1B_/2B_4. B8B/2B-/"8. D6D8DEFG

52. IN COELESTIBUS REGNIS, A & ORCHESTRA   XVII/1:34
     (A tempo guisto, #FC, C) '2DF/8A4A6B"C4D'D/

53. IN HAC DIE, SSATB & ORCHESTRA   XVII/1:38
     (Allegro moderato, #FC, C) "4DD6FE4. D/'6A"8. C6E8. G

DOUBTFUL WORKS:

54. ?   9/1057
     PRO JESU DUM VIVO, SA & ORCHESTRA   XVII/1:101
     (Allegro non presto, #FCG, C) "8E/4E3D6. C3F6. E8DC

55. ?   9/1057
     VEXILLA REGIS, SATB & ORCHESTRA   XVII/1:138
     (Andante, bBEAD minor, ¢) '2A4AA/AG2G/2. F4F/1nE/

H. Jacob[?]

Twelve

SONATAS

For Two

VIOLINS and a BASS

or an

ORCHESTRA

Compos'd by

GIO. BATT.ᴬ PERGOLESE.

AUTHOR of the STABAT MATER.

The Manuscripts of these Sonatas were procured by a Curious Gentleman of Fortune, during his Travels through Italy.

LONDON.

Printed and fold by R. BREMNER, facing Somerfet-Houfe in the STRAND.

Title page, *Twelve Sonatas, Two Violins and Continuo.*
Washington: Library of Congress, Nos. 12-23.

SPURIOUS WORKS:

56. X   9/1057
     ADORO TE DEVOTE, S & ORCHESTRA   XVII/1:1
         (Andante, bBEAD minor, 3/4) "6C/8. F6C4C8. -6A/8. G

57. X   9/1057
     AVE VERUM, S & ORCHESTRA   XVII/1:12
         (Andante sostenuto, #F, 3/4) '4GAB/EA"C/'F2G/

58. X Durante, Francesco   9/1057
     DORME, BENIGNE JESU, S & ORCHESTRA   XVII/1:29
         (Andantino, #F, 12/8) "2. D_8. D6C'8B "4E8F/gA4. G_

59. X Durante, Francesco   9/1057
     MAGNIFICAT, SATB & ORCHESTRA   XVII/1:66
         (Allegro moderato, bBE, C) '2B_4. B"8C/4. D8D2D/D

60. X   9/1057
     O SACRUM CONVIVIUM, SATB & ORCHESTRA   XVII/1:97
         (Andante sostenuto, bB!, C) 2-'G/"lbE_/2E4DC/'B"C2D

61. X   9/1057
     SISTE, SUPERBE FRAGOR, B & ORCHESTRA   XVII/1:121
         F-4 clef (Comodo, #F, C) '8D, B6-B'CD8D, G4-/

62. X   9/1057
     SUPER FLUMINA BABYLONIS, SATB & ORCHESTRA   XVII/2:1

     a. Super flumina babylonis
         (Largo, bBE minor, C) "2DE/4. D8E2D/4. nE8G4G#F/
     b. In salcibus (S solo)   9
         (Andante, #F, 2/4) 4-8G6"GD/gD8. C6C4B/
     c. Quia illic interrogaverunt (S solo)   15
         (Allegro assai, #FC, C) 2-"D/'BG/D4A"8DE/4. F
     d. Hymnus cantate   20
         (Allegro assai, #FC, C) 4A8EA6BAB"C'B"CD'B/4"C
     e. Si oblitus fuero tui (SS duet)   29
         (Andantino,   , 3/8) "4C8C/4. D/E/'8. A"6F(EDC)/8C'B-/
     f. Memento Domine   37
         (Adagio, bBE minor, 6/8) '4. B"C/C'4nB8B/"4. C4C8#C/4D

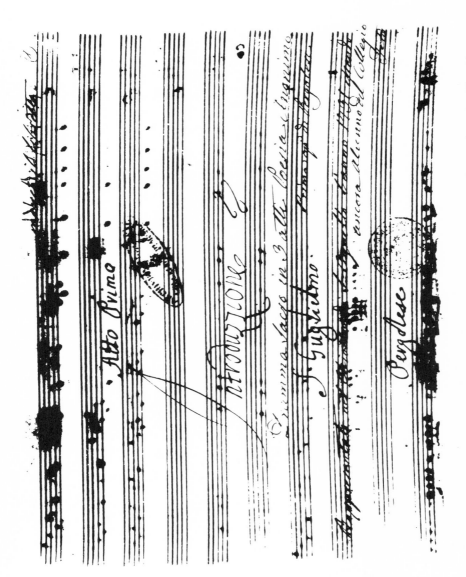

Title page, *Guglielmo d'Aquitania.* Naples: Biblioteca del Conservatorio. No. 63.

Oratorio and Sacred Drama

AUTHENTIC WORK:

---

p. E' dover che le luci (T solo)   82
    (Maestoso, bBE!, C) 2-"8GGE6DE/8CC
q. A sfogar lo sdegno mio (B solo)   88
    F-4 clef (Moderato, bBEA, 2/4) ,4EE/8E'4E8C_/C,4B8A/G
r. Lascia d'offendere (S solo)   92
    (Andante, bBE, 3/4) '4B"DF/'4. G8#F4G
s. Viat'isso! viat'isso! Siente di (B solo)   95
    F-4 clef (, #F, ₵) 2.-,8.G6G/4GD-8.B'6C/4D,G
t. Vola al ciel, anima bella (SB duet)   99
    (Largo, #FC, C) "6DEFG8AG6FE4D8-/

DOUBTFUL WORK:

64. ?
    LA MORTE DI S. GIUSEPPE (oratorio)   I:1
a. Sinfonia
    (Allegro moderato, #FC, C) "4DD8.D6F8EG/gG8F6EDgF8E

    ACT I
b. Innalziam lodi al signore (S solo)   5
    (Allegro spiritoso, #F, C) '4GB"4.D6C'B/"8CDEFG'G
c. Se a tanto fuoco (T solo)   9
    F-4 clef (Larghetto, , 3/4) '4G8FEDC/,6BA4. G
d. Muoiono le fenici (S solo)   14
    (Allegro spiritoso, #FC, C) "2D4FG/gFG2A_8AGFE/6DC8. D
e. Appena spira l'aura soave (S solo)   17
    (Andante, bB, C) 2-'4F8AB/"gD6C'nBgB4. C
f. Soave ferite (A solo)   22
    (Allegro moderato, #FCG, 2/4) 4.-8B/E"C'6BGAF/E
g. In te ripone il cor (T solo)   26
    F-4 clef (Larghetto, #F minor, C) 4.-'8D,G3B6.G'3D,6.B'8G
h. Pellegrin che in cupo orror (A solo)   30
    (Allegro spiritoso, bBEA, C) 1'E/B/"2E4-E/DC'BA/2G
i. Il signor vuol ch'a me solo (AT duet)   36
    F-4 cleg (Larghetto, , C) 2-'4.G8E/gD4C8-CDEgG4F/E
j. Dolce auretta ch'alletta (T solo)   41
    F-4 clef (Andantino, #F, 3/8) ,4.G/'gCD4.E/8DC,B/'C,BA
    ACT II
k. Già in te rinascere (S solo)   45
    (Allegro spiritoso, #FC!, C) 2-8-'A"CD/8.E'6E4E
l. Pastorello in mezzo ai fiori (A solo)   49
    (Andantino, bB, 3/8) '6.F3A8GE/6.F3A8GE/6F"8DC'6B/3AG
m. Vola intorno al primo raggio (S solo)   53
    (Allegro grazioso, bBE, C) 2-'6B"CDEFDEC/'2B
n. O buon pastor (SST trio)   58
    (Larghetto, bB, 3/4) 2-"4C/'8.A6GgG2F
o. Sposa, và: verrà quel di (A solo)   64
    (Allegro spiritoso, #FC, C) 2-'8AD4-/B8-F4G8-A/4D
p. L'ardor che cresce in seno (T solo)   68
    F-4 clef (Largo, bBEA minor!, C) '8C/FFFF6nED8C

22

Psalms

AUTHENTIC WORKS:

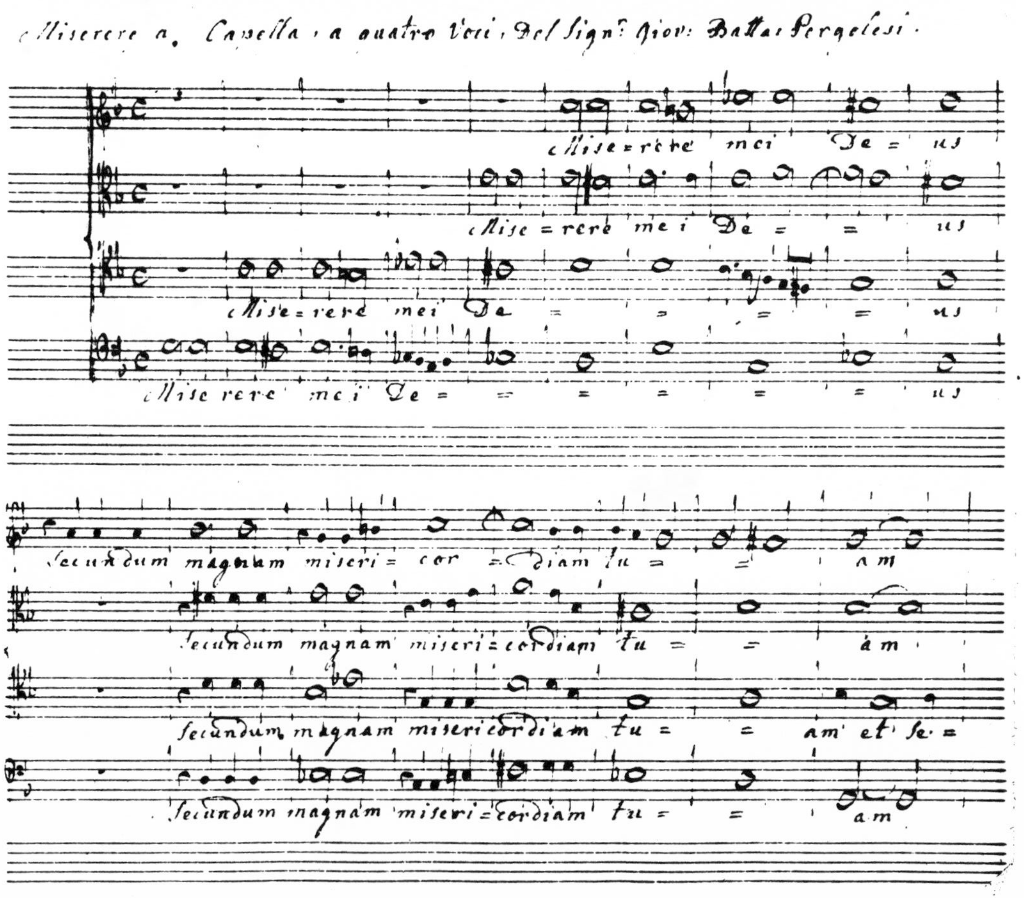

First page, *Miserere mei.* London: British Museum. No. 347.

71.   ?   8/410
      MISERERE MEI, DEUS, SATB & ORCHESTRA   XIII:77

   a. Miserere mei, Deus
         (Largo, bBEA minor, C) '2BB/G#F/nBB/1bA/G/
   b. Et secundum multitudinem (SATB quartet)   82
         (Andantino, bBEA, 3/8) '4.B/"C/'6BA8G-/-BB/"gC'8BGAG
   c. Tibi soli peccavi (T solo)   89
         (Allegro moderato, bBE, 2/4) '4B"C/6DC'8B-"D/6C'A8F
   d. Ecce enim in iniquitatibus (A solo)   93
         (Andante, bB, 3/4) 4-'2F_/8F6EF4GE/FC-/
   e. Ecce enim veritatem dilexisti   96
         (Adagio, bB minor, C) "4D#CDE/DD8DD#CD/#CC
   f. Asperges me hyssopo (S solo)   99
         (Larghetto, bBE minor, 2/4) "8D/gC'8B6AG"gF8E6DC/8#FG
   g. Auditui meo dabis gaudium (ATB trio)   103
         (Allegro, bBE, C) '8F4B8BA/BFGABFGA/B
   h. Averte faciem tuam (A solo)   108
         (Andantino, bB, 3/8) '8FGA/DGB/EF-/
   i. Cor mundum crea in me, Deus (B solo)   111
         F-4 clef (Andante molto sostenuto, bB minor, C) , 8A/4DE6FG
   j. Ne projicias me a facie tua   115
         (Allegro moderato, bBE, 3/4) 4-'BA/4.B8A4B/2A4B/GAB/BA
   k. Domine, labia mea aperies (B solo)   123
         F-4 clef (Andante, bBEA minor, 3/4) , 8CEF/GnAnB/'C, G'E
   l. Quoniam si voluisses   126
         (Adagio assai, bBE minor, C) "4.C8C4C/8-CCCCCC/4.C8C
   m. Sacrifium Deo (ATB trio)   128
         (Adagio, bBE!, C) '4EEE8DD/2.E4D/E
   n. Benigne fac (S solo)   130
         (Larghetto, bBEA minor, C) '8G"C4E8D/6C'nB"8C
   o. Tunc acceptabis sacrificium   134
         (Largo, bBEA, C) '4A8AABBBB/8.B6B8BB8.bA6A4A

SPURIOUS WORKS:

72.   X   9/1057
      BEATUS VIR QUI TIMET, SATB & ORCHESTRA   VIII:213

   a. Beatus vir qui timet
         (Allegro moderato, bB, C) 2.-"4C_/C'nB"8C'CEF/
   b. Gloria Patri   229
         (Largo, bB!, C) '4.A8A2A/"4D8DD4.C8C/'4B

73.   X Leo, Leonardo   9/1057
      DIXIT DOMINUS, DOMINO MEO, SSATB, SSATB   8/410
      & ORCHESTRA   VIII:113

   a. Dixit Dominus, Domino meo (SSATB)
         (Allegro spiritoso,   , ¢) '1G_/G/A/G/"2.C4C/1C/

b. Donec ponam (S solo)   122
    (Andante, #F, C) "8D'G_6. G3B6. A3G"gCD8E4D
c. Virgam virtutis (S solo, SSA̅TB)   126
    (Spiritoso, #FC, ₵) "1D/2ED/DD/DC/D-/
d. Tecum principium in die (A solo)   133
    (Andante grazioso, #FC minor, C) '8B4F8#A6BF4F8B/B
e. Juravit Dominus (SSATB)   137
    (Largo, #F, C) "2DD/(D)8-DDD/2C_8C'B"4C/gC'4BGA(-)
f. Dominus a dextris tuis (SSATB solo)   151
    (Allegro, #FC, C) '8AF4D_8D6EF8GG/FA4. D
g. Gloria Patri (SSATB)   158
    (Largo, bB!, 3/4) '4. B8B4B/1-/-/"4. D8D4D/4. D8D4D/
h. Sicut erat (SSATB)   160
    (Spiritoso, , C) '1G/G/A/G/"C/C/2CC/2. D4D/1C

From:
Laudate pueri Dominum, S, SATB & ORCHESTRA
(No. 65)

i. Quis sicut Dominus   252
    (Andante, bBEA, 3/4) '2. E/"E/gD2. C/gC'8. B6E4E-/

74.   X   9/1057
    SANCTUM ET TERRIBILE, SSATB & ORCHESTRA   VIII:207
    (Andante, minor, 3/4) "2E4E/2E4E/8. E6E4E

Sequences and Antiphons

AUTHENTIC WORKS:

75.   SALVE REGINA, S & STRINGS (2 VIOLINS &   XV/1:1
    CONTINUO), A minor

a. Salve regina
    (Largo, minor, C) '2A8B"DC'B/"C'BA
b. Ad te clamamus   3
    (Allegretto, , 3/8) "8CEG/6C'B"4C/6DC4D/
c. Ad te suspiramus   4
    (Larghetto, , C) '8B/"CG4-8EG-D/EG
d. Eia, ergo   5
    (Allegretto, bB, 3/8) "4. F/C/'8AGF/"DEF/C'BA/
e. O clemens, o pia   8
    (Largo, minor, C) "8CC'B-"D/DC-E#CbBAC/6D#C8D

76.   SALVE REGINA, S & STRINGS (2 VIOLINS &   XV/1:34
       CONTINUO), C minor

   a. Salve regina
      (Largo, bBEA minor, C)   2-"C_/4C'nB"2E/8. D3EF8ED6ED
   b. Ad te clamamus   36
      (Andante, bBE minor, C)   '8G/"2DD/1D_/D/2D4-'8G/"2GG/1G
   c. Ad te suspiramus   38
      (Largo, bBEA minor, C)   "8D/gC'4. nB"8A4. G8G/gF4F
   d. Eia, ergo   40
      (Andante, bB minor, 2/4)   "2D/E/4. F8D/E6FG8FE/
   e. Et Jesum   43
      (Andante un poco mosso, bBE, 3/4)   '4B/"2. F/E/D/4CDE/D
   f. O clemens, o pia   46
      (Largo, bBEA minor, C)   "8CC'nB-"D/DC-C2bD/C

77.   STABAT MATER, SA & ORCHESTRA   XXVI:1

   a. Stabat Mater
      (Grave, bBEAD minor, C)   2-'G_/4GF2B_/4BA"2D_/4D
   b. Cuius animam (S solo)   4
      (Andante amoroso, bBEA minor, 3/8)   "8C4D/8E4F/8G4A
      (same music as no. 80b)
   c. O quam tristis   7
      (Larghetto, bBE minor, C)   "4DD#CD/2-4nCC/C'B
      (2-part version of no. 80d)
   d. Quae moerebat (A solo)   9
      (Allegro moderato, bBEA, 2/4)   '8E4E6FG/8F4F6GF/
      (same music as no. 80e)
   e. Quis est homo   12
      (Largo, bBEA minor, C)   "4. C8E6DCgC4D8-/4DG8nE
      (2-part version of no. 80f)
   f. Vidit suum dulcem Natum (S solo)   15
      (Tempo guisto, bBEAD minor, C)   "4C3F6. E3D6. C/8D4. C
      (same music as no. 80g)
   g. Eia Mater (A solo)   18
      (Allegro moderato, bBEAminor, 3/8)   '8GED/6C, nBgB'4C/
      (same music as no. 80h)
   h. Fac ut ardeat   21
      (Allegro, bBE minor, ¢)   "1D/E/2. D'4B/"C'A"DC/'2BG/
   i. Sancta Mater   27
      (Tempo giusto, bBEA, C)   2-"E/'B6EDgD4. E/
      (2-part version of no. 80i)
   j. Fac ut portem (A solo)   34
      (Largo, bBE minor, C)   '4G_6. G3B6. A3G8#F"g#C8D
      (same music as no. 80j)
   k. Inflammatus et accensus   37
      (Allegro non troppo, bBE, C)   "8F4F8ED4D8C/'t4B"tC6DC'8B

l. Quando Corpus morietur   41
    (Largo, bBEAD minor, C) "4CFFnE/2-4F'A/AG
    (same music as no. 801)
m. Amen   44
    (Presto assai, bBEAD minor, ₵) "1C/D/C/'B/2A4BAt1G/2F
    (2-part version of no. 80m)

DOUBTFUL WORKS:

78. ?   9/1057
    SALVE REGINA, SS & STRINGS   XV/1:17

a. Salve regina
    (Largo, bBEAD minor, C) 2-"4CC/F'F8-6G"D8. C
b. Mater misericordiae   20
    (Andante, bBE, 3/8) '8B_3B"C'BA8B/F#FG_/
c. Ad te clamamus   22
    (Largo, bBEA, C) "2EE_/8.E3DC'8BAGF4(E)/
d. Eia, ergo   25
    (Allegro, bBE minor, 2/4) "4DE/'#FG/8.E6ED"C'BA/
e. Et Jesum   28
    (Andante, bBEA minor, 2/4) "4. C6GE/'4nB"C/8.D3EF8ED/
f. O clemens, o pia   31
    (Largo, bBEAD minor, C) '4B8-B/BA4-B8-B/BA-A2A/4(G)

SPURIOUS WORKS

79. X   9/1057
    SALVE REGINA, SB & STRINGS   XV/1:10

a. Salve regina   10
    (Larghetto, bBEA minor, C) "4ED8C6DE8DC/4C'nB
b. Ad te clamamus   11
    (Andantino, bBEA, C) '4B8BB/"4Ξ'E8-"C'BA/8. G
c. Eia, ergo   13
    (Allegretto, bBE minor, 2/4) "4DE/gE4. D8E/D6C'B"8C'6BA/
d. Et Jesum   14
    (Larghetto, bBEA minor, 3/4) '4G/"CDE/FED/8ED4C-/
e. O clemens, o pia   15
    (Largo, bBEA minor, C) "8C'nB"CDC/C'nB-

80. X   9/1057
    DIES IRAE, SATB & ORCHESTRA   XXVI:47

a. Dies irae
    (Largo,   , C) "4C'G"8CCC'B/"CCC'B"6CD8E
b. Quantus tremor (S solo)   52
    (Andante amoroso, bBEA minor, 3/8) "8C4D/8E4F/8G4A/'8nB
    (same music as no. 77b)

SECULAR VOCAL MUSIC
Chamber Arias

AUTHENTIC WORKS: None

DOUBTFUL WORKS:

81. ?
      AH SE SOFFERSI, O DIO, A & STRINGS   18/304
         (Andante, bB, C) '8F6EF8GCgFG8AG   XXII:27

82. ?
      PENSA, SE AVRŎ, MIA CARA, S & STRINGS   18/304
         (Andantino, bB, 3/4) '2. F/4A2F/"4C'2A/"4DC-/   XXII:18

83. ?
      SI CANGIA IN UN MOMENTO, A & STRINGS   18/304
         (Allegro vivace,   , 3/8) "4. C/'6BAt4G/8GAB/"C'C   XXII:32

SPURIOUS WORKS:

84. X
      AH, CHE SENTO IN MEZZO AL CORE, B & STRINGS   18/307
         F-4 clef (Allegro spiritoso, bBEA, C) ,2. E4E/BB-B/'2. E4E   XXII:93

85. X
      AMERŎ FINCHĔ IL MIO CORE, A & STRINGS   18/304
         (Allegretto, #FCGD, C) 4-'8BG2E/4. -6GA8BG"C'B/"C'B   XXII:35

86. X
      BENDATO PARGOLETTO, A & CONTINUO   18/305
         (Allegretto, bBEA, C) ,8B'6EDED8EF/4GF   XXII:59

87. X
      CARA, TU RIDI, A & CONTINUO   18/305
         (Andante, bB!, C) '4G8. D6G4#FG/A8-A8. A   XXII:65

---

88. X Galuppi, Baldassare   18/306
      CHI NON CREDE ALLE MIE PAROLE, S & STRINGS   XXII:86
      (Spiritoso, #F, C) '6GA/8B6B''C8D6GE8ED

89. X   18/303
      EMPIO AMOR, AMOR TIRANNO!, S & STRINGS   XXII:1
      (Allegro, bBE, C) '2B/F4.B''8D/4ECD'8B

90. X Bononcini, Antonio   18/304
      E PUR VER, A & STRINGS   13/540
      (Allegretto, #F, C) '4AD/B8-AGF4G/F   XXII:24

91. X   18/305
      INGRATA NON SARŎ, A & CONTINUO   XXII:61
      (Larghetto, bB minor, 12/8) 4-'8A4.BA-/-4-8BAGF4F8E

92. X Leo, Leonardo   18/307
      IO NON SO DOVE MI STO, B & STRINGS   13/540
      F-4 clef (Allegro, bBEA, C) , 4.E8F4.G8A/B'C,ABG'C XXII:88

93. X Scarlatti, Alessandro   18/304
      NON MI TRADIR, A & CONTINUO   13/540
      (Larghetto, bB minor, 12/8) '4.A6G8F4G8A4.D4 XXII:43

94. X   18/304
      PENSA BENE, MI DICESTI, A & CONTINUO   XXII:41
      (Allegro, #FC, 3/4) '8FG4AA/BFG/A8BAGF/2E4D/

95. X   18/305
      PER ESSER PIŬ VEZZOSE, A & CONTINUO   XXII:57
      (Andantino, bBEA, C) '8EDC,B'D/EFGEDC

96. X   18/305
      PER VOI MI STRUGGO IN PIANTO, STB & CONTINUO XXII:98
      (? , bB!, ₵) 2-''D_/DC_/C'B_/BA_/A4GF/1bE/2D

97. X   18/304
      PIANGERŎ TANTO, A & CONTINUO   XXII:50
      (Lento, bBEA minor, 3/4) '4G8AG4F/G2C/

98. X Lampugnani, Giovanni Battista   18/303
      QUAL DOLENTE PASTORELLO, S & STRINGS   13/540
      (Largo, bBEA, C) '8.G6A/8BEE''EC'B-   XXII:10

99. X Bononcini, Antonio   18/304
      QUANDO BASTI A FAR MORIRE, A & STRINGS   13/540
      (Allegro moderato, #FCGD, C) '4.E6DE/4.F6EF4.G6FG XXII:30

100. X   18/304
      QUANT' INGANNI INSEGNA AMORE, A & CONTINUO   XXII:46
      (Allegro, #FC, 3/4) '4FG/4.A8G4F/GGF/2E4E/

101. X Aresti, Floriano   18/304
      SE AMOR TI COMPOSE, A & CONTINUO   13/540
      (Allegro, #F, 3/8) '8D/6GFGFGF/8GDD/   XXII:39

102. X   18/303
      SENTIR D'UN VAGO OGGETTO, S & STRINGS   XXII:6
      (Andantino, #FCG, 3/8) "8E/'A_6.A"3C'6.B"3D/gD8C_6.C

103. X Lampugnani, Giovanni Battista   18/304
      SENTIRSI IL PETTO ACCENDERE, S & STRINGS   16/295
      (Larghetto, bB, 2/4) "8C/6C'AGF8F"F/6DC8C   XXII:15

104. X Bononcini, Antonio   18/305
      SE PER TE VIVA IO SONO, A & CONTINUO   13/540
      (Allegro moderato, bBEA, C) '8B6AG8FE/F,B   XXII:63

105. X Parisotti, Alessandro   18/305
      SE TU M'AMI, S & STRINGS   9/1055
      (Andantino, bBE minor, 2/4) "4D6E8.C/4C6D8.B/   XXII:68

106. X Ciampi, Vincenzo Legrenzio (?)   7/432
      TRE GIORNI SON CHE NINA, S & STRINGS   13/540
      (Andantino, bBE minor, C) '4G/"DDDE/ED-E/ED-   XXII:66

107. X   18/304
      UN CIGLIO CHE SÀ PIANGERE, A & CONTINUO   XXII:48
      (Vivace, #FCGD, 3/4) '4E/4.B8A4G/A2B/4.G8F4E/

108. X Bononcini, Antonio   18/304
      VANNE A SEGUIRE, A & CONTINUO   13/541
      (Andantino, #FC, C) '4D8.F6G4A8.D6A/8GFED   XXII:55

109. X   18/304
      VORREI POTER ALMENO, A & CONTINUO   XXII:52
      (Andante mosso, bBE minor, 12/8) '8DGABAB"C/'4B8A4.G

Chamber Cantatas

  d. Cadrò contento dal duolo oppresso   40
       (Allegro, bBEA, 2/4) '6B/"4E'B/6GF8E4-/"8E'4E8D/

DOUBTFUL WORKS: None

SPURIOUS WORKS:

118. X   18/306
        COR PRIGIONIERO, S & STRINGS   XXII:70

  a. Cor prigioniero che, vaneggiando
       (Amoroso, #FCG, C) '8A6B"C'8B"6CDEDE'B/8CA
  b. Non sperare dai fieri incanti   72
       (Allegretto, #FC, 3/4) //:"4D2E/4F8EF4D/FED/C
  c. Sareste pur care   73
       (Allegro, #FCG, 3/8) "8E//: 6ED8CF/6ED8CF/6ED8C

Fragments of Operas

AUTHENTIC WORK:

119. MO CHE TE STREGNO, SB DUET   XIX:supp.
        F-4 clef (Larghetto, #F, 3/8) ,gB'C8D6C,BAG/'C,AgA4B/

DOUBTFUL WORKS:

120. ?   18/307
        SERBI L'INTATTA FEDE, S & STRINGS   XIX:9
          (Andante mosso, #FC, C) "2D4DD/2.D4F/4DD-F/

121. ?   18/307
        TU RESTERAI, MIA CARA, SS & STRINGS   XIX:77
          (Andantino, bB, C) "8C/FCCD6(D'CB)gB"8C

122. ?   18/307
        VA TRA LE SELVE IRCANE, S, HORNS & STRINGS   XIX:16
          (Allegro non troppo, bBE, C) '2B4FD/2G4.F8G/gF2E4D

SPURIOUS WORKS:

123.   X   Chinzer, Giovanni   18/307
       AH! MI DIVIDON L'ANIMA, GLI ACERBI AFFANNI   16/295
       MIEI, S & STRINGS   XIX:1
       (Andante spiritoso, bBEA minor, C) "4C8. G6F/4ED8. C

124.   X   Di Capua, Rinaldo   18/308
       BASTA, COSÌ TI INTENDO, S & STRINGS   13/540
       (Allegro moderato, bBE, C) '4B"gD8C'6BAgA4B   XIX:38

125.   X   Vinci, Leonardo   18/308
       CONFUSA, SMARRITA, S & STRINGS   9/1055
       (Con moto, bB minor, C) '8A/"D'D-A6BA8G-   XIX:34

126.   X   Sellitti, Giuseppe   18/308
       DEH, T'ACCHETA E NON NEGARMI, SS & STRINGS   16/295
       (Un poco andante, #F, C) "4D8-'G6AFgF8G-G/6AF4D   XIX:71

127.   X   Scarlatti, Giuseppe   18/307
       IMMAGINI DOLENTI PERCHÉ NEL COR TI   13/540
       STANNO ? S & STRINGS   XIX:5
       (Andante, #F, ¢) '4G/"8. D6E8. D6E8D#DEF/

128.   X   18/308
       MISERO ME, QUAL GELIDO TORMENTO,   XIX:42
       RECITATIVE, S & STRINGS
       (Andante mosso,   , C) "8D'6AA/4#F8-DDDDD/4#FF

129.   X   18/308
       NON SO DONDE VIENE, B & STRINGS   XIX:51
       F-4 clef (Andante, bBE, 3/4) ,8F/4B'4. F,8A/BA4B

130.   X   18/307
       NON TI MINACCIO SDEGNO, S & STRINGS   XIX:29
       (Andante, #FCG, 3/8) "8E6DC'BA/"8EFG/A'A-/

131.   X   Orlandini, Giuseppe Maria   18/308
       SE MI LASCI, O MIO CONTENTO!, SS & STRINGS   7/1055
       (Andante, bBE minor, C) "4. D'8G"3D#C8. D6-'AB"C/   XIX:62

132.   X   18/308
       SO CH'È FANCIULLO AMORE, B & STRINGS   XIX:47
       F-4 clef (Allegro moderato, #FC, C) '4D8-gFE8DD/6. D3C8D-D

133.   X   Terradellas, Domenico   18/308
       TALOR SE IL VENTO FREME, S & STRINGS   13/540
       (Assai spiritoso, #FC, C) '8A/"4D'DFA/"2. D_8D6FE   XIX:55

Title page, *La serva padrona*. Naples: Biblioteca del Conservatorio. No. 137.

134. X Giay, Giovanni Antonio   18/308
      TU NON RISPONDI, INGRATO, SS & STRINGS   7/1055
      (Larghetto, #F, C) "8D3D'6. B3A6. G"3E6. C'3B6. A/

135. X Terradellas, Domenico   18/307
      TU VUOI CH'IO VIVA, SS & STRINGS   13/541
      (Comodo, bB, 2/4) '8C/6FAA"CCFFC/g'B"C8DC   XIX:22

136. X Orlandini, Giuseppe   18/308
      UNA POVERA FANCIULLA, SB & STRINGS   XIX:82
      (Allegro, #F, 3/8) '8B"C/4D8E/4D8C/'BG"E/4D

Intermezzi

AUTHENTIC WORKS:

137. LA SERVA PADRONA   XI/1:1
   a. Sinfonia (X)*
      (Presto assai, bB, C) "6F/4F8-6FG8FAFA/4F

      ACT I:
   b. Aspettare e non venire (B solo)   5
      F-4 clef (Allegro moderato, bBE, C) ,4BB2B_/B,,4B-/,DC,,B
   c. Quest è per me disgrazia (Recitative) (B solo)   8
      F-4 clef (! , , C) '8D,6AA8#FAAD-6AA/
   d. Stizzoso, mio stizzoso (B solo)   17
      (Allegretto, #FCG, 2/4) '8A//"4ED/8C'ABG/AE-
   e. Lo conosco a quegliocchietti (SB duet)   24
      (Allegro, #F, C) 4.-'6B"C8D'G-6B"C/8D'G"GED'G

      ACT II:
   f. A Serpina penserete (S solo)   36
      (Larghetto, bBE, 2/4) 4.-"DE/8F'B"8C6. D3E/DC'8. B
   g. Son imbrogliato io già (B solo)   43
      F-4 clef (Tempo giusto, bBEA, C) 8-,BGE'C,FGD/E
   h. Contento tu sarai (SB duet)   51
      (Allegro spiritoso, #FCG, 3/8) 4-"8E/ECD/EAE/FE-/

138. LIVIETTA E TRACOLLO   XI/3:1

---

*Only the sinfonia is spurious.

INTERMEZZO I:
a. Vi sto ben? (S solo)   1
    (Allegro, bBE, C) '6. F3F/4B6-F6. F3F8"CC
b. A una povera polacca (B solo)   5
    F-clef (Larghetto, bBE minor, 3/8) ,8G4G/8G#FG/'3E6. C8B
c. Sarebbe bella questa (S solo)   14
    (Allegro, !, C) '8A/B"CD'G#FA-A/
d. Ecco il povero Tracollo (B solo)   18
    F-4 clef (Recitativo, !, C) ,8. A6D4D-8-D/8. G6G8GD4E-/
e. Vado, vado ! (SB duet)   23
    F-4 clef (Allegro, #F, C) '8D, G4-'8D, G4-/8-BAG

INTERMEZZO II:
f. Vedo l'aria che s'imbruna (B solo)   32
    F-4 clef (Allegro moderato, #F, C) ,2GB/'8D, G4-2E/DC/4B
g. Caro, perdonami (S solo)   38
    (Andante, bBE, 2/4) "8D'G-B/6AG8A4-/"'D'A-
h. Non si muove, non rifiata (B solo)   41
    F-4 clef (Tempo giusto, , C) ,8D/AG4. -8GGD/FE
i. Sempre attorno qual colomba (SB duet)   50
    (Presto, #FCG, 3/8) '8A"C'B/A"DC/'BAG/A"C'B/

139. LA CONTADINA ASTUTA   XI/2:1

FROM INTERMEZZO II:
a. Per te ho io nel core (SB duet)   38
    (Allegro moderato, #FC, C) '8A/"8. D3C'B8A#G4A8A/

SPURIOUS ARIAS:
INTERMEZZO I:
b. X Hasse, Johann Adolph   18/309
   Alla vita, al portamento (B solo)   13/540
   F-4 clef (Tempo giusto, #F, 3/8) '8D,BG/gG4F8G/'CC   XI/2:1
c. X Hasse, Johann Adolph
   Sul vago praticello (SB duet)   4
   (Andante, #FCG, 2/4) 4. -'8A/"4. E8D/4C_6CABE/8A4A
d. X Hasse, Johann Adolph
   Più vivere non voglio (S solo)   10
   (Allegretto, minor, C) 4. -"8EC'AE#G/A"C
e. X Hasse, Johann Adolph
   Vorrei . . . oh Dio ! ma vedo (SB duet)   16
   (Andante, #F, C) "8D/'6BA8G-BBA"C/C'B-

INTERMEZZO II:
f. X Hasse, Johann Adolph
   Belle e cocenti lacrime (S solo)   28
   (Adagio, #F, C) "8D3C'BAG"8GE
g. X Hasse, Johann Adolph
   Ah perfida ! E poi trattarmi così (B solo)   33
   F-4 clef (Allegro, #FC, C) ,8A/8. F6E8D'D6C'B8A-
   Per te ho io nel core
   (SEE No. 139a)

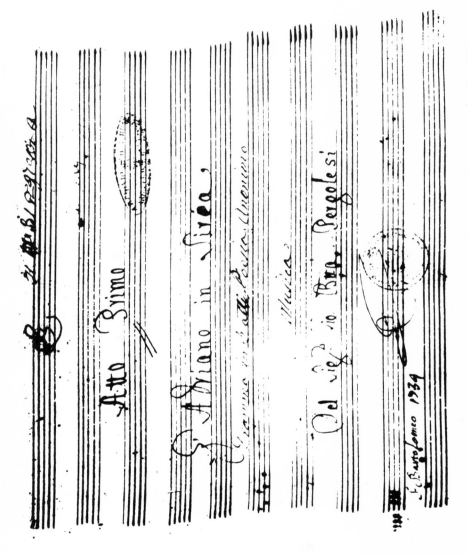

Title page, *Adriano in Siria*. Naples: Biblioteca del Conservatorio. No. 140.

DOUBTFUL WORKS: None.

SPURIOUS WORKS: None.

Operas

AUTHENTIC WORKS:

140.   ADRIANO IN SIRIA   XIV: 1

  a. Introduction
      (Allegro assai e spiritoso, #FC, C) 8♩'DDDDDDD/DDDDD6C'B

     ACT I:
  b. Dal labbro che ti accende (T solo)   10
      (Amoroso, #FCG!, C) '8E/6GEAFBG''C'A''8#D4E
  c. Sprezzo il furor del vento (Bar solo)   15
      F-4 clef (Allegro spiritoso, bB, 3/4) ,4FA'C/F,2F/8FE2F
  d. Sul mio cor so ben qual sia (T solo)   27
      (Allegro spiritoso, #FC!, C) 2-'A/''AgA4.#G8F/4ED6CB8A
  e. Prigioniera abbandonata (S solo)   38
      (Tempo giusto, #FC, C) '4.A6(FED)4.B''6(DC'B)/
  f. Vuoi punir l'ingrato amante? (T solo)   43
      (Andante, bBE, ₵) '2B''C/gC2.D4E/4.F6ED4CB
  g. Chi soffre senza pianto (S solo)   47
      (Larghetto ma con moto,   , C) ''8G/4.C8G4.D8G/6.E3F8G-
  h. A un semplice istante (Bar solo)   56
      F-4 clef (Allegro moderato, bBEA, C) ,8B'2E/,4.B8AGE-,,B
  i. Sola mi lasci a piangere (S solo)   65
      (Tempo giusto, bB, C) 2-''8C6FF8F''D/8.D6C8C
  j. Lieto così talvolta (T solo)   68
      (Amoroso,   , C) 2-''4C6CDE#F/g#F4.G

     ACT II:
  k. Ah, ingrato, m'inganni (S solo)   80
      (Andantino, bBE minor, 2/4) ''4D8-'B/gA6G#F8G-B/
  l. Saggio guerrier antico (T solo)   85
      (Tempo giusto, bB, C) '2F4.A6GF/''4CF6ED8C4D_/
  m. Splenda per voi sereno (S solo)   91
      (Allegro,   , C) 2-''G/4.D8C'6BA8G''4E/8D'G-

m. Quel morzelletto cannarutetto (TB duet)   63
    F-4 clef (Allegro assai, #F, 3/8) ,8GBA/B'6D,B'C,A/8G4A

ACT II:
n. Amor che si sta accolto (T solo)   71
    (Allegro, #F, 3/8) '8G3B6. G3C6. A/"3D6. B4E
o. La sciorte mia è accussì barbara (T solo)   77
    (Andante, bBE!, 2/4) "8G4C8D/8. E6D4C/
p. In mezzo a questo petto (S solo)   81
    (Spiritoso, #FC, C) '8D/FDFA"D'D-
q. Io son d'un animuccio (S solo)   85
    (Allegro, , C) '8G/"CCCDE4E8F/
r. Del fiero tuo dolore (T solo)   90
    (Andante, bBE minor, C) 4. -'8GgC8B6AG"gC'8B6AG/"6E#C4D
s. Da rio funesto turbine (S solo)   94
    (Allegro agitato, #FC, C) 2-'D/4FA"2D/F8. A6A4A
t. Quanno voi vi arrossegiate (B solo)   101
    F-4 clef (Andante con motto, , C) 2-'4. C,8A/GA4. G8AGEgG
u. Se spiego i sensi miei (ST duet)   106
    (Tempo giusto, #F, C) 4. -'8D8. G3AB"8CC/C'6. B
v. Cacciatemi, cacciatemi (STB trio)   113
    (Allegro moderato, #F, C) "8D/gC'8. B6A8G"DgC'8. B6A8GB/

ACT III:
w. Queste fronde e questi sassi (T solo)   120
    (Andante, bB, C) '6AB/"8C'F-"C4. D6(FED)/6CD8C-
x. Sta barca desperata (T solo)   123
    (Allegro spiritoso, #FC, C) '8A/"D6FE8DDgE6DC4D8A/
y. L'oggetto del cor mio (S solo)   127
    (Amoroso, #FCG!, C) '8E/3G6. E3A6. F3B6. G"8CC'B   ·
z. Ad annientarmi potea discendere (S solo)   130
    (Allegro assai, #F, C) '4G8B"D4G'8G"G/FEDC'BAG
aa. Chi ha il cor fra la catene (T solo)   134
    (Amoroso, bBE, C) 4-'8FF4. B"8D/gD4. C8C6DE4F
bb. Non abbia più riposo (T solo)   139
    (Allegro, #F, C) '8G/BGB"DG'G-"D/ECGEDG-
cc. Per te ho io nel core (SB duet)   144
    (Allegro moderato, #FC, C) '8A/"8. D3C'B8A#GGAA/
dd. Ite a godere ch'io non v'invidio (SSSTTB sextet)   153
    F-4 clef (Allegro, #FC, 3/8) '8DFE/g#6DC4D/,8B'G,B/B4A/

142. IL MAESTRO DI MUSICA   XXV:1
    (SEE No. 148 for spurious arias)

    FROM ACT I, SCENE 3: Variant
a. Son timida fanciulla (S solo)   67
    (Allegretto, bBE, 2/4) '8F/BBBB/"6DC'8B-

    FROM ACT II:
b. Non vo'più dargli ascolto (S solo)   45
    (Allegro, #F, C) '8G/4BGB"D/G'8G
c. Venite, deh siate gentile (ST duet)   51
    (Allegretto, bBE, 3/8) '8B/"6. D3E8FE/DGF/F4E/D

Title page, *Il prigionier superbo*. Naples: Biblioteca del Conservatorio. No. 143.

143. IL PRIGIONIERO SUPERBO   XX:1

  a. Introduction
     (Allegro spiritoso, #FC, C) "8FAFAFAFA/4F-2-/

    ACT I:
  b. Splenda il sol di luce adorno (Chorus)   6
     (Allegro, #FC, 6/8) "4. DF/8EDC'BAG/6FE8D
  c. Premi, o tiranno altero (Bar solo)   10
     F-4 clef (Presto, , C) 2-'4C8E#F/4G, G'6C, B'8C-
  d. Che fiero martire (B solo)   16
     F-4 clef (Andante, #FCGD, C) ,8E/B4A8GgAB'8C4B
  e. Fra tanti affanni miei (A solo)   20
     (Larghetto, #F minor, C) 4-'8B/B"C'B/B"C'B/6A#G4A/
  f. Parto, non ti sdegnar (T solo)   24
     (Larghetto, bBE, C) "8FD4. -'8B"gCD8. E6DC/8B
  g. M'intendeste? non pavento! (A solo)   31
     (Largo, bB, C) 4-'8. A6F"8CC4-/-8. D'6F8GG
  h. Un aura di speranza (T solo)   39
     (Allegro assai, #FC!, ¢) "4E/'A2. A/gB"C2. D8C'B/4A2. A/
  i. Giusti numi che scorgete (S solo)   43
     (Amoroso, bB, C) "2FC/'6AG4. F"8DFgbE4D/C
  j. Salda quercia allor che incalza (Bar solo)   52
     F-4 clef (Allegro spiritoso, #FC, C) 2-, D/A'8D, D-'D/4G, B8BA

    ACT II:
  k. Se il tuo labbro chiede vendetta (T solo)   57
     (Allegro, , 2/4) "8C4C8E/#CD4-/8D4D8F/#DE
  l. Serba per altri rai quell'alma infida (S solo)   63
     (Allegro moderato, bB, 6/8) '8FAGFBA/4. F'F/
  m. Del mio valore al lampo (T solo)   69
     (Allegro, #FC, C) 4. -'8A"D6FE8D'A/FD
  n. Trucidati a queste piante (B solo)   79
     F-4 clef (Presto, bBEA, C) ,2EG/4BE'EC/, BE
  o. Vado a morte: a te la figlia lascio (Bar solo)   84
     F-4 clef (Andante, bBE, C) ,4BFgE8. D6C, 4B/8-'GEGGF
  p. Chi mi sgrida? (A solo)   94
     (Andante, bBEA, 3/4) '2. EB"4E'E-/2. -/, B'F/4B, B-/

    ACT III:
  q. Ombre mute, oscuri orrori (T solo)   99
     (Largo, bBEA, C) 2-'E/E6EDgD4. E/8-FGA
  r. Dopo il periglio de la tempesta (T solo)   107
     (Allegro ma non troppo, bB, 3/8) '8F3A6. F3B6. G/"8CCF
  s. Padre. Non vò ascoltarti (ATBar trio)   111
     (Allegro moderato, bBE, C) 2-'4BF/1-/-/"4C'F2-/1-/4-"4. C
  t. Vedi, ingrato (S solo)   121
     (Moderato, #FC!, C) 2-'A/"E4A'8AC/4B" 'CD
  u. Volgi a me vaghe ciglia (AB duet)   129
     F-4 clef (Andante amoroso, , C) ,8GG/'3C, 6. B3A6. G3F6. E
  v. Trema il cor, s'oscura il ciglio (B solo)   135
     F-4 clef (Allegro, bBEA, C) 2-'E/, B4E8-,,B, /2C,, 4. B

First page, *Sinfonia, Lo frate 'nnamorato.* Naples: Biblioteca del Conservatorio. No. 144a.

Title page, *L'Olimpiade*. Naples: Biblioteca del Conservatorio. No. 145.

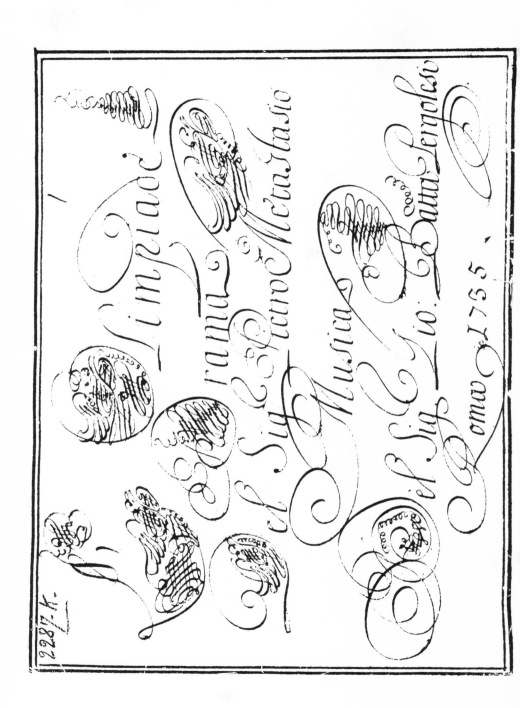

L'Olimpiade Drama Per Musica Del Sig. Pietro Metastasio

Musica del Sig. Gio: Batta Pergolesi

Roma 1755

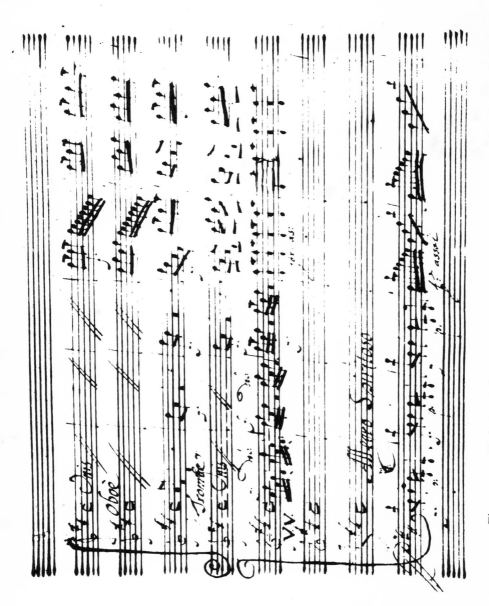

First page, *Sinfonia*, *Salustia*. Naples: Biblioteca del Conservatorio. No. 146a.

DOUBTFUL WORKS: None

SPURIOUS WORKS:

i. X Auletta, Pietro
   Quando sciolto avrò il contratto (T solo)   33
      (Allegro, bBE, 2/4) 4-"8FE//:DC'BA/BF
j. X
   Se giammai di speco l'eco (S solo)   37
      (Allegretto, #FCG, C) "4CD8EEEE/FE4-8FE
k. X
   Splende fra noi seren di pace (Chorus)   39
      (Allegro moderato, , C) "8E4E8DC4C8C/D4C'8B"6C'B4C
l. X
   Qual dopo insano nimbo (SA duet)   42
      (Andantino, #F, 12/8) "8DCD'4B"8CDCD'4.B/
m. X
   Mio caro signor Maestro (STB trio)   57
      (Allegro moderato, #F, 2/4) '8G/"D4D8E/'FA-"C/'B4A

THEMATIC LOCATOR
Works in Opera Omnia Transposed to C Major or C Minor

      As mentioned above, the 659 musical incipits in the <u>Opera Omnia</u> have been transposed and alphabetized through the use of two computer programs. The note sequence for alphabetization is as follows:

Ab A A# Bb B B# Cb C C# Db D D# Eb E E# F F# Gb G G#

Column one is the incipit transposed to C major or C minor.

Column two is the catalogue number (and letter where applicable).

Column three gives the genre, using the following code

Ar	Chamber Aria	Of	Fragment of Opera
Ca	Chamber Cantata	Op	Opera
Cn	Concertino	Or	Oratorio or Sacred Drama
Co	Concerto	Ps	Psalm
In	Intermezzo	Sa	Sequence or Antiphon
Ma	Mass	Si	Sinfonia
Mf	Fragment of Mass	So	Sonata
Mo	Motet	Su	Suite

Column four refers to the authenticity of the work: ? (doubtful) or X (spurious). The absence of ? or X indicates that the authenticity of the work has not been challenged.

Column five gives the key: capital letters for major keys, lower case for minor keys. Where the key signature is incomplete or inappropriate, the implied key of the opening bars is used as a guideline, and an asterisk is appended.

AbAbGGAbGG	45a	Ma		f*	CCBAGFEDC	78c	Sa	?	Eb
					CCBCCCCBCC	26b	Cn	?	G
ABCCBC	41	Co	X	C	CCBCDF	12c	So	?	G
					CCBCEDFE	144a	Op		D
BbAAABBBCC	48j	Ma	X	C	CCBCGE	26a	Cn	?	G
BbBbBbBDDC	49a	Ma	X	D	CCBCGG	70e	Ps	?	c*
BbBBBBbBBA	50g	Ma	X	Bb	CCBDDCCDbC	76f	Sa		c
BbEbGEbBbG	64g	Or		e	CCBEADGC	50c	Mo	X	Bb
					CCBEEF	46a	Mo	?	D
BCBCGGAAC	49g	Ma	X	D	CCBGABC	65g	Ps		D
BCDEFGC	30c	Cn	?	Eb	CCBGFE	25a	So	?	C
BCGEGDEG	75c	Sa		C	CCCBbCCCDb	39	Mf	?	b
					CCCBAGAFGE	145i	Op		F
CAbGFEbFGG	60	Mo	X	g*	CCCBAGFEDC	140d	Op		A*
					CCCBB	47a	Ma	?	F
CAEDCC	63c	Or		G	CCCBBCBC	71m	Ps	?	Eb*
CAFCGCDE	62c	Mo	X	D	CCCBBCDEF	143q	Op		Eb
CAFDGFEG	30b	Cn	?	Eb	CCCBCAbFEb	138b	In		g
CAGAGAGEGF	141t	Op		C	CCCCAbF#F	146l	Op		g
CAGBbGF	67d	Ps	?	d	CCCCAAA	491	Ma		D
					CCCCAGFEC	63q	Op		Eb
CBAGAAG	27a	Cn	?	G	CCCCBEEEED	70k	Ps		Eb
CBAGAAGCD	67e	Ps	?	G	CCCCAGCAG	64q	Or		G
CBAGAFEDC	28d	Cn	?	A	CCCCBBCDB	48i	Ma		C
CBAGFEDCAG	147j	Op	X	F	CCCCCCCB	48f	Ma	X	d
CBAGFEDC	5b	Su	?	D	CCCCCCCBC	144gg	Op		D
CBAGGABCC	83	Ar	?	C	CCCCCCCCC	144m	Op		D
CBAGGGFGA	501	Ma	X	Eb	CCCCCCCCCC	140a	Op		D
CBBAAG#	49f	Ma		D	CCCCCGFED	3d	Su	?	E
CBBCCBGAG	48h	Ma		C	CCCCCDEbD	26c	Cn	?	E
CBBCCCBb	70m	Ps		c	CCCCCEDECE	145a	Op		D
CBCBGCE	32c	Co		F	CCCCCEDECE	63a	Or		D
CBCDBCG	71d	Ps		F	CCCCCGEDC	69g	Ps	?	C
CBCDCCB	79e	Sa	X	c	CCCCECCE	120	Of	?	D
CBCDCCCBC	71e	Ps	?	d	CCCCEDCGG	137b	In		Bb
CBCDCDEDEF	99	Ar	X	E	CCCCGABbC	48a	Ma	X	C
CBCDEFGG	148g	Op	X	Bb	CCCCGCGC	144x	Op		A*
CBCDGCDED	81	Ar	?	F	CCCDCDD	14b	So	?	Eb
CBCGCBCG	144g	Op		c*	CCCDCECEC	137a	In		F
CBEDEFEDED	76a	Sa		c	CCCDEbDCCC	144b	Op		g
CBGADGCB	16c	So	?	C	CCCECDCFC	27b	Cn	?	G
					CCCEDFFEDC	64a	Or		D
CCBAAGCC	73i	Ps	X	Eb	CCCEECCDG	49b	Ma	X	D
CCBABG	13b	So	?	Eb	CCCEEEDEF	27b	Cn	?	G
CCBAGFED	69e	Ps	?	Eb	CCCEEGGCCC	113e	Ca		Eb
					CCCEGCG	48b	Ma	X	C
					CCCGABCC	146cc	Op		D
					CCCGEFGC	63s	Or		G

NB: Column 1 = incipit; 2 = catalogue number; 3 = genre; 4 = authenticity; 5 = key.

CCCGGFEDCB	113d	Ca		A	CDEDCEDCGG	148b	Op	X	C
CCDbDCBC	70c	Ps	?	g	CDEDCEFGFE	69a	Ps	?	C
CCDCBbCD	69b	Ps	?	a	CDEDECEDCB	118b	Ca	X	D
CCDCECFC	26d	Cn	?	G	CDEDEFGFGD	118a	Ca	X	A
CCDDEED	66a	Ps	?	C	CDEDFEDEDC	144z	Op		Eb
CCDDEED	66g	Ps	?	C	CDEEEEEE	59	Mo	X	Bb
CCDEAFEDCC	62e	Mo	X	C	CDEEEEEE	50a	Ma		Bb
CCDEDDED	77d	Sa		Eb	CDEEFGCAAG	88	Ar	X	G
CCDEDDED	80e	Sa	X	Eb	CDEFDECC	65e	Ps		C
CCDEEFGFE	144c	Op		G	CDEFEDEC	46g	Ma	?	C
CCDEFEDCB	49k	Ma	X	G	CDEFFEED	28b	Cn	?	A
CCDEFGAGF	23c	So	?	E	CDEFGABCC	49h	Ma	X	D
CCDEF#F#G	140j	Op		C	CDEFGAFGEA	92	Ar	X	Eb
CCECGG	141f	Op		D	CDEFGAGFED	17c	So	?	D
CCEC#DDDF#	143k	Op		D	CDEFGCBAGF	116c	Ca		Eb
CCEDCGBDFE	53	Mo		D	CDEFGEFDC	64m	Or		Bb
CCEDFEGFED	35c	Si		G	CDEFGFEDC	63t	Or		D
CCEDF#AGG	146z	Op		f	CDEFGGGF	23a	So	?	E
CCEGAG	144ff	Op		F	CDEFGG#AA	68d	Ps	?	G
CCEGAGCGFE	140u	Op		F	CDEF#F#GG	146v	Op		F
CCFDBCBCGF	49j	Ma	X	A	CDFEbDEbDC	75a	Sa		a
CCFECAGGF	144d	Op		F	CDFEDCCGA	67b	Ps	?	Bb
CCGFEDCBAA	110b	Ca		F					
CCGFEEDC	24b	So	?	Eb					
CCGGAAEEF	3c	Su	?	E	CEbDCBF#G	77j	Sa		g
CCGGABbBAA	114a	Ca		F*	CEbDCBF#G	80j	Sa	X	g
CCGGABCCC	63g	Or		F	CEbDCCCBC	141b	Op		d
CCGGCCGG	69c	Ps	?	C	CEbDCCDDG	80f	Sa	X	c
CCGGFFE	62b	Mo	X	G	CEbDCCDDG	77e	Sa		c
CCGGGCCBG	84	Ar	X	Eb	CEbGCEbCGC	28c	Cn	?	f#
CDCBCDCGEC	147a	Op	X	G	CECBAGFED	63j	Or		D
CDCBCGBB	5c	Su	?	D	CECEGCC	141p	Op		D
CDCBCGG#A	78b	Sa	?	Bb	CECEGCC	142b	Op		G
CDCCCCBC	73c	Ps	X	D	CECEGCCGA	141bb	Op		G
CDCDEFGAGF	114c	Ca		F	CECFDGEA	141n	Op		G
CDCEEDF	45g	Ma		Bb	CECFDGEAAG	141y	Op		E*
CDDEbFGAb	111c	Ca		b	CECFDGEABC	141ee	Op		G
CDDEFGFEEC	140f	Op		Bb	CECFDGEAFB	140b	Op		E*
CDEbCDEbF	76d	Sa		d	CECFDGGC	143r	Op		F
CDEbCEbGCB	33b	Co	?	e	CECGEAG	82	Ar	?	F
CDEbCFEbDC	18c	So	?	g	CECGECGE	141i	Op		Eb
CDEbFEbD	70b	Ps	?	g	CECGED	19c	So	?	Eb
CDEbFGAbBC	77b	Sa		c	CECGGGFEC	20a	So	?	A
CDEbFGAbBC	80b	Sa	X	c	CEDBCEDBCA	641	Or		F
CDEADFBC	71h	Ps	?	F	CEDCBAGFED	143b	Op		D
CDEADFBC	57	Mo	X	G	CEDCBBC	124	Of	X	Bb
CDEDCEDBG	71c	Ps	?	Bb	CEDCCCBCC	132	Of	X	D

NB: Column 1 = incipit; 2 = catalogue number; 3 = genre; 4 = authenticity; 5 = key.

CEDCDEFE	45b	Ma		C
CEDCDGG	70d	Ps	?	Eb
CEDCEDCEDC	148c	Op	X	A
CEDCFECC	143 l	Op		F
CEDCGCBAG	140q	Op		Eb
CEDCGCBAG	145v	Op		Eb
CEDCGCBAGA	140 l	Op		F
CEDCGCEG	145s	Op		D
CEDCGFED	70j	Ps	?	Eb*
CEDCGFGG	48e	Ma	X	F
CEDCGGG	66c	Ps	?	Bb
CEDDCBCAFA	141dd	Op		D
CEDDEGEAG	145f	Op		D
CEDEGEG	35a	Si	?	G
CEDEGEFDCD	141m	Op		G
CEDGDCCBD	65d	Ps		C
CED#CFED#C	138i	In		A
CEEDGG	141k	Op		D
CEEEDCGFG	146n	Op		D
CEFAGDF#G	64e	Or		F
CEFEFGFED	64d	Or		D
CEFGABC	49e	Ma	X	D
CEFGABCBAG	146o	Op		F
CEFGABCC	144ii	Op		Eb
CEFGABCCGE	71k	Ps	?	c
CEFGAGCC	146k	Op		Eb
CEFGCBAG	146i	Op		A
CEFGCBAG	148h	Op	X	G
CEFGCGFEDC	108	Ar	X	D
CEFGEDCBC	146c	Op		D
CEFGFEAGGF	142c	Op		Bb
CEFGF#G	144y	Op		A*
CEFGGCCBBC	115c	Ca		F
CEFGGG	148a	Op		Bb
CEFGGGCBAG	33a	Co	?	G
CEF#GFGFED	144o	Op		G
CEF#GGCBC	143c	Op		C
CEGAAAG	63k	Or		Bb
CEGAABAG	145g	Op		Bb
CEGAG#A	63r	Or		Bb
CEGABCC	10	So	?	Bb
CEGCAGFE	138f	In		G
CEGCBAG	7	So	?	Bb
CEGCBC	8	So	?	G
CEGCBCDCD	75b	Sa		C
CEGCBAGCBA	30d	Cn	?	Eb
CEGCCAGC	143n	Op		Eb
CEGCCBAGA	65c	Ps		G
CEGCCBAGFF	145d	Op		D
CEGCCCBAGF	141z	Op		G
CEGCCCBAGF	146r	Op		Eb
CEGCCCBC	145c	Op		F
CEGCCBC	140c	Op		F
CEGCEGGG	141s	Op		D
CEGCEGGGF	144s	Op		D
CEGCGAAAAG	147m	Op	X	D
CEGFEABCC	63t	Or		D
CEGFEFGABC	64b	Or		G
CEGGABCC	52	Mo		D
CEGGFEGCC	20c	So	?	A
CFDEAG	144n	Op		F
CFDGEAA	144aa	Op		G
CFEbDCFEbD	141r	Op		g
CFEAGFF	42	Mf	X	G
CFEDCGFCAG	141d	Op		E*
CFEFEFGAG	86	Ar	X	Bb
CFGAGFEFED	64j	Or		G
CFGGCC	144jj	Op		D
CGAbAbGFEbD	146t	Op		e
CGAAAAG	114b	Ca		Bb
CGABbCDBC	48 l	Mo	X	C
CGABCCBCDE	117a	Ca		Eb
CGAGABC	12a	So	?	G
CGAGAGG#AB	127	Of	X	G
CGAGDFAAG	146m	Op		D
CGAGFFE	45c	Ma		G
CGAGGAGG	18b	So	?	Eb
CGBCAFGC	68f	Ps	?	Bb
CGBCGGCF	73d	Ps	X	b
CGCBBC	77i	Sa		Eb
CGCBBC	80i	Sa	X	Eb
CGCBC	113h	Ca		d
CGCBCDD	87	Ar	X	g*
CGCCBAGFE	64h	Or		Eb
CGCCCAFGC	144g	Op		Eb
CGCCCBB	38	Ma		D
CGCCCBCCCB	80a	Sa	X	C
CGCCCFAAG	143j	Op		D
CGCCEDEF	143t	Op		A*
CGCCEDGFED	146y	Op		G
CGCCGDGG	143p	Op		Eb
CGCDECDCBC	146b	Op		D
CGCDFEDCBC	146s	Op		G

NB: Column 1 = incipit; 2 = catalogue number; 3 = genre; 4 = authenticity; 5 = key.

CGCDGDE	145l	Op		C	CGCGFFE	49c	Ma	X	A
CGCEFDE	89	Ar	X	Bb	CGGGAbAbG	106	Ar	X	g
CGCGAG	143v	Op		Eb	CGGGABCC	146j	Op		E
CGCGECG	4b	Su	?	E	CGGGAFFDFG	110a	Ca		Eb*
CGCGGCAA	144e	Op		D	CGGGCAG	13a	So	?	Bb
CGDGDBAGF	143s	Op		Bb	CGGGEDCDCB	145j	Op		Ab
CGEbCGC	144k	Op		c	CGGGFEDDCB	31a	Cn	?	Bb
CGEbDCCGEb	63l	Or		d	CGGGGEE	45e	Ma		D
CGEbFEbDC	24a	So	?	g	CGGGGGC	76b	Sa		g
CGEAGAGFE	122	Of	?	Bb					
CGEBCDEFED	78e	Sa	?	c					
CGECAG	36c	So	?	Bb	C#AG#FEC#E	31b	Cn	?	Bb
CGECCDEFG	25c	So	?	C	CEBAG#BC#D	95	Ar	X	Eb
CGECGE	50d	Ma	X	Bb	C#EDC#G#FG	65b	Ps		Bb
CGECGEC	33c	Co	?	G					
CGECGFEDEF	145bb	Op		D	DAAF#DDDDD	128	Of	X	C
CGEDCABCGF	75d	Sa		F	DAGGGDFE	138h	In		C
CGEDCACBbA	143i	Op		F					
CGEDCACBC	113c	Ca		Bb	DCBAGGF	76c	Sa		c
CGEDCAFGEF	67h	Ps	?	D	DCFEbAb	77a	Sa		f
CGEDCBAG	145w	Op		F					
CGEDCBDGBD	15c	So	?	G	DDCBCDCGF	15b	So	?	C
CGEDCC	63c	Or		G	DDDDDBBB	112a	Ca		D*
CGEDCCGEDC	80c	Sa	X	C					
CGEDDCBC	141g	Op		c	DGEDBCAG	64f	Or		A
CGEDDEFD	46c	Ma	?	Bb	DGFEGEDG	23b	So	?	E
CGEDEFGFED	1	So	?	A*					
CGEDGFE	21c	So	?	F	EbCGEbDCCC	29a	Cn	?	f*
CGEFDCBC	63n	Or		F					
CGEFGAGCC	19b	So	?	Bb	EbDCCGAbBC	37b	Si	X	d
CGEFGBDCBC	115b	Ca		Eb	EbDDDbCC	46f	Ma	?	c
CGEFGGC	116b	Ca		Eb	EbDEbDEbD	71j	Ps	?	g
CGFEbAbG	50i	Ma	X	f	EbDEbEbEb	43	Mf	X	a
CGFEbDCDD	16b	So	?	a					
CGFEbDEbCF	63i	Or		c					
CGFECDGCC	139c	In	X	A	EbEbDFFEbG	75e	Sa		a
CGFEDCAFAA	143o	Op		Bb	EbEbEbDCBB	117c	Ca		c
CGFEDCAGC	140m	Op		G	EbEbEbDDD	66f	Ps	?	c*
CGFEDCBC	123	Of	X	c	EbEbEGGGGG	73g	Ps	X	g*
CGFEDEC	67a	Ps	?	D					
CGFEDEC	17a	So	?	D	EBbAbBEDC	70g	Ps	?	g
CGFEDEGE	76e	Sa		Bb					
CGFEFGAG	143d	Op		E	ECCCCCCGED	34b	Co	?	D
CGFEFGEDC	107	Ar	X	Eb	ECDEFDEC	48d	Ma	X	C
CGGAAAG	145o	Op		D					
CGGABCBAGF	143w	Op		D					
CGGABDFED	148m	Op	X	G					
CGGEGGCGG	137c	In		D*					

NB: Column 1 = incipit; 2 = catalogue number; 3 = genre; 4 = authenticity; 5 = key.

63

Incipit	Cat.	Genre	Auth.	Key
ECEF#G#FE	32b	Co	?	F
ECGGACDD	143g	Op		F
ECGGGAF#F#	144bb	Op		Eb*
ECGGGCECG	63e	Or		A
EDCBAGFEF	30a	Cn	?	Eb
EDCCD	46h	Ma	?	D
EDCDEDCCB	79a	Sa	X	c
EDDC#CC	68e	Ps	?	C
EDEDCDBCBC	64r	Or		D
EEDCCCDCBC	148k	Op	X	C
EEDEFEDEA	146dd	Op		D
EEECCCCCB	68a	Ps	?	D
EEECCCFEC	140w	Op		D
EEEDDEC#C	46d	Ma	?	C
EEEEDDCCB	55	Mo	?	f
EEEGGEDC	68c	Ps	?	D
EEEGGGABCB	51	Mo		G
EEEGGGG	68g	Ps	?	F
EEFEFGGG	40	Mf	X	G*
EEFGFEFGGE	5a	Su	?	D
EFCCBCBBB	70h	Ps	?	Eb
EFDGGAFE	46b	Ma	?	G
EFEDCCB	67g	Ps	?	D
EFEFGECDEE	47b	Ma	?	D
EFFEEFF#FG	62f	Mo	X	g
EFGAGFECAG	136	Of	X	G
EFGCCAFGC	144hh	Op		G
EFGCCCAG	98	Ar	X	Eb
EFGCDEFEDC	137f	In		Bb
EFGCEFGCCA	137e	In		G
EFGCGACBAG	141w	Op		F
EFGFEDCFDD	119	Of		G
EFGFEFFEDD	100	Ar	X	D
EFGGAEFG	94	Ar	X	D
EFGGCAAG	147h	Op	X	F
EFGGGEDCFE	147l	Op	X	F
EFGGGGABCC	31d	Cn	?	Bb
EFGGGGAGAG	148j	Op	X	A
EF#GGDbEFF	50f	Ma	X	g
EF#GGEF	47f	Ma	?	c*
EGABCDEFGA	37a	Si	X	D
EGEGEGEGE	143a	Op		D
FFAbGCBbAb	35b	Si	?	d
FFFEbFFFEb	78f	Sa	?	f
FFFFFFFFFF	711	Ps	?	g
FFFGGGGGGG	71o	Ps	?	Eb
F#GABbAGG	144cc	Op		f#
GAbAbGAbGF	79c	Sa	?	g
GAbBbCBbC	29c	Cn	?	f
GAbBCAbAGF	78d	Sa	?	g
GAbFFGEb	105	Ar	X	g
GAbGAbGFEb	91	Ar	X	d
GAbGAbGF#G	144j	Op		e
GAbGBCEbFD	24c	So	?	g
GAbGCGCGFD	36b	So	?	g
GAbGEbFDGF	77h	Sa		g
GAbGFEbFEb	80m	Sa	X	f
GAbGFEbFEb	77m	Sa		f
GAbGFGC	97	Ar	X	c
GAbGGGFFEb	66d	Ps	?	g
GABCBAAGFF	145e	Op		F
GABCCDC	48g	Ma	X	G
GABCCDEDDE	34a	Co	?	D
GABCCGAGGF	116a	Ca		Eb
GABCFDEC	68h	Ps	?	D
GABCFEGG	138c	In		D*
GAFEFF	147f	Op	X	g
GAFGFEEFDE	67f	Ps	?	G
GAGAGACCB	62a	Mo	X	g
GAGCGFFE	145u	Op		A
GAGFEGGAG	71b	Ps	?	Eb
GBACBCDC	70a	Ps	?	c
GBCAbGF#G	29d	Cn	?	f
GBCGBCC	145p	Op		c
GCAbBGF	22c	So	?	d
GCAbGFEbDC	47c	Ma	?	b
GCACBC	17b	So	?	G
GCAEFGC	64o	Or		D

NB: Column 1 = incipit; 2 = catalogue number; 3 = genre; 4 = authenticity; 5 = key.

GCAGFEAGFE	36a	So	?	Bb	GCDEFFFE	141u	Op		G
GCAGFCFE	90	Ar	X	D	GCDEFGAGA	146e	Op		E*
GCBbAbGAbG	77f	Sa		f	GCDEGFEDCB	144h	Op		Bb
GCBbAbGAbG	80g	Sa	X	f	GCDEbFEbD	79d	Sa	X	c
GCBAGAbAbG	116d	Ca		c	GCDGAGCBC	146p	Op		F
GCBAGF#FGG	141cc	Op		D	GCEbDCBCDC	144r	Op		d
GCBAGF#GG	139a	In		D	GCEbDCDGD	138g	In		g
GCBCAbG	12b	So	?	e	GCECGAGFFD	21a	So	?	F
GCBCBCBCGG	101	Ar	X	G	GCEDCBC	71n	Ps	?	c
GCBCDC	9	So	?	C	GCEDCCCC	16a	So	?	C
GCBGDCDEbD	70l	Ps	?	g	GCEDCCDCBC	141x	Op		D
GCCBAbG	141dd	Op		f	GCEDCDEE	144p	Op		G
GCCBCEbEbD	77l	Sa		f	GCEDCFGAG	73b	Ps	X	G
GCCBCEbEbD	80l	Sa	X	f	GCEDCGEC	143m	Op		D
GCCBCGABC	71g	Ps	?	Bb	GCEDFE	144l	Op		Bb
GCCBDDFEbD	117b	Ca		f*	GCEDFEDCBC	146h	Op		Bb
GCCCAAGG	140i	Op		F	GCEDFFEG	102	Ar	X	A
GCCCBAGFGA	146bb	Op		Bb	GCEEDFEFG	141e	Op		Bb
GCCCCBAG	64p	Op		f*	GCEEDG	3a	Su	?	E
GCCCCBAG	146w	Op		F	GCEEGGCCGF	135	Of	X	F
GCCCCBC	145z	Op		C	GCEFGABCC	140t	Op		D
GCCCCBC	63d	Or		E	GCEGCDFAD	22b	So	?	Bb
GCCCCCBCCD	112c	Ca		C	GCEGCGCEGC	146a	Op		D
GCCCCCGAGC	144v	Op		F	GCGABCC	146f	Op		F
GCCCCCGFED	2	So	?	F	GCGBCBC	129	Of	X	Bb
GCCCCEDC	142a	Op		Bb	GCGCEDC	138e	In		G
GCCCDCD	144w	Op		c*	GCGCEED	20b	So	?	D
GCCCDEbGF	31c	Cn	?	g	GCGDGEFG	140g	Op		C
GCCCDEEF	141g	Op		C	GCGEbAbF#G	45f	Ma		g
GCCCDFEE	111a	Op		C	GCGEbDCGF#	146d	Op		e
GCCCEFGEFD	145r	Op		Bb	GCGECAGG	144t	Op		Eb
GCCCFFFCD	138d	In		d*	GCGECCC	15a	So	?	G
GCCDEFEDCC	143h	Op		A*	GCGECCGECC	147d	Op	X	D
GCCDFEEFA	146g	Op		Bb	GCGECGG	140p	Op		D
GCCDFEGDFE	148d	Op	X	D	GCGECGG	145x	Op		Bb
GCCEGCED	133	Of	X	D	GCGEDCCCB	117d	Ca		Eb
GCCGAbGFF	125	Of	X	d	GCGEDCGBC	146aa	Op		C
GCCGGAAGC	140n	Op		F	GCGEDCGC	141h	Op		G
GCCGGF#GAC	29b	Cn	?	f	GCGEFEDG	19a	So	?	Eb
GCDBBCCDBG	126	Of	X	G	GCGFECGAG	140h	Op		Eb
GCDDEDDECD	147k	Op	X	G	GCGFEDC	145b	Op		G
GCDDEE	32a	Co	?	F	GCGFEFD	141c	Op		G
GCDEbDC	141o	Op		c*	GCGFEFG	63b	Or		G
GCDEbDCBCB	70f	Ps	?	g	GCGGFEEDCA	11a	So	?	F
GCDEbDEbF	109	Ar	X	g	GCGF#GDEbF	131	Of	X	g
GCDEbFG	14a	So	?	c	GCGGAAGFFG	121	Of	?	F
GCDEbFGAbG	71i	Ps	?	d	GCGGAGFED	13c	So	?	Bb
GCDEDCC	65a	Ps		D	GCGGAGGCG	143x	Op		G

NB: Column 1 = incipit; 2 = catalogue number; 3 = genre; 4 = authenticity; 5 = key.

incipit	catalogue	genre	auth	key
GCGGCGAGCA	113a	Ca		A*
GCGGEbDGG				
GCGGFEFG				
GDGAGABAB	62d	Mo	X	D
GEbCGBCEb				
GEbDCBBC	77g	Sa		c
GEbDCBBC	80h	Sa	X	c
GEbDCBCEb	140k	Op		g
GEbDCDDB	34c	Co	?	d
GEbDCEbDB	68b	Ps	?	b
GebDCEbEbF	46e	Ma	?	e
GEbDCGFGAb	67c	Ps	?	d
GEbFDEbGC	27c	Cn	?	e
GEbFGAbFG	49d	Ma	X	f#
GECADEBC	137g	In		Eb
GECBCCAGC	146x	Op		Bb
GECBCDFEDG	148e	Op	X	G
GECBCEFGG	144u	Op		Bb
GECCBCFF	139b	In	X	G
GECDEEDCB	6	So	X	C
GECDEFEDC	143f	Op		Bb
GECDEFFEGC	73f	Ps	X	D
GECDEFGAFG	146u	Op		A
GECDGG	144i	Op		C
GECGCBCD	147e	Op	X	G
GECGCBGG	145n	Op		D
GECGGFE	50b	Ma	X	Eb
GEC#EFGEAG	85	Ar	X	E
GEDCACBA	140e	Op		D
GEDCACBA	145t	Op		D
GEDCACGC	66b	Ps	?	G
GEDCCBAG	139g	In	X	D
GEDCCBAG	141j	Op		g
GEDCCCBDD	145y	Op		G
GEDCCDEGFE	64i	Or		C
GEDCCEbEDD	66e	Ps	?	Eb
GEDCEEDFFE	139e	In	X	G
GEDCEFEF	147i	Op	X	Eb*
GEDCGCBAG	113g	Ca		Eb
GEEDDC	64n	Or		F
GEEFGGC	61	Mo	X	G
GEFDEC	28a	Cn	?	A
GEFGEC	141l	Op		Bb
GEFGEFGFGA	141a	Op		D

incipit	catalogue	genre	auth	key
GEFGGEFG	145k	Op		D
GFEbDAbBb	71f	Ps	?	g
GFEbDCAb	22a	So	?	d
GFEbDCAbG	145m	Op		g
GFEbDCBbAG	96	Ar	X	g*
GFEbDCBC	18a	So	?	g
GFEbDCBC	47e	Ma	?	e
GFEbDCCF#G	145q	Op		g
GFEbEbDEbB	65f	Ps		g
GFEbFGCG	93	Ar	X	d
GFEABDC	58	Mo	X	G
GFECDBCG	137d	In		A
GFECFDGE	4c	Su	?	E
GFEDCAG	140o	Op		E*
GFEDCBAG	64c	Or		C
GFEDCBCG	148i	Op	X	Bb
GFEDCCA	139f	In	X	G
GFEDCCCCC	115a	Ca		F*
GFEDCDG	104	Ar	X	Eb
GFEDCED	37c	Si	X	D
GFEDCEDCBC	3b	Su	?	E
GFEDCEDCD	145h	Op		Bb
GFEDCGABCC	130	Of	X	A
GFEDCGEED	140v	Op		G
GFEDCGFEDC	141v	Op		G
GFEEDC	32d	Co	?	F
GFEEED	34d	Co	?	D
GFEFDEDC	140r	Op		Bb
GFEFGGFE	140s	Op		G
GFEFGGFE	110c	Ca		Eb
GFFEbCAbGG	50j	Ma	X	D
GFGAbBbAbG	44	Mf	X	d
GFGAGAG	49i	Ma	X	G
GFGAGFEDCC	48k	Ma	X	G
GFGAGGE	148f	Op	X	G
GFGCGABCG	112b	Ca		G
GFGEFGFGE	148l	Op	X	G
GF#GDCBCBb	70i	Ps	?	c*
GF#GGBC	72a	Ps	?	F
GGAbAbAbAb	45d	Ma		e*
GGAbGGAbGF	143e	Op		e
GGAABBAbG	71a	Ps	?	c
GGABCGAFDG	63m	Or		D
GGAGCCC	73a	Ps	X	C

NB: Column 1 = incipit; 2 = catalogue number; 3 = genre; 4 = authenticity; 5 = key.

GGAGCCCDD	73h	Ps	X	C	GGEDCAFED	134	Of	X	G
GGAGFEDEDC	147g	Op	X	E	GGEDCCCAGG	103	Ar	X	F
GGAGFEED	50k	Ma	X	Bb	GGEFGCC	113b	Ca		A*
GGBCDGDEF#	69d	Ps	?	C	GGEFGCGAG	137h	In		A
GGBCGGC	45h	Ma		F	GGFEAGFEAG	118c	Ca	X	A
GGCACBCD	14c	So	?	c	GGFEAGFEC	54	Mo	?	A
GGCBAGFEDC	143u	Op		C	GGFEEDCD	77k	Sa		Bb
GGCBAGG	47g	Ma	?	G	GGFEEDCD	80k	Sa	X	Bb
GGCBCAB	70n	Ps	?	c	GGF#GFFFEb	77c	Sa		g
GGCBGCG	21b	So	?	d	GGF#GFFFEb	80d	Sa	X	g
GGCCBCC	145aa	Op		Eb*	GGGAFDCB	48c	Ma	X	G
GGCCCDBCEb	146g	Op		A	GGGCBAAG	144f	Op		E*
GGCCDAbG	78a	Sa	?	f	GGGCCAGFE	79b	Sa	X	Eb
GGCCDBbBBB	113f	Ca		Eb	GGGCCCBB	72b	Ps	X	D*
GGCCEbD	147c	Op	X	c*	GGGGF#F#G	47h	Ma	?	F
GGCEEDDEFG	141aa	Op		Bb	GGGGF#G	47d	Ma	?	G
GGCCEbDCC	69f	Ps	?	c*	GGGGABC	4a	Su	?	E
GGCGGGCG	50e	Ma	X	Bb	GGGGGGFEFF	73e	Ps	X	G
GGCGGGDD	138a	In		Bb	GGGGGGG	74	Ps	X	a
GGEbDEbCC	63p	Or		c*	GGGGGGGC	25b	So	?	f
GGEbFGG	63h	Or		c	GGGGGGGGGF	50h	Ma	X	Bb
GGEDC	63o	Or		A					

NB: Column 1 = incipit; 2 = catalogue number; 3 = genre; 4 = authenticity; 5 = key.

INDEX TO
THEMATIC CATALOGUE
Composers, Titles, and First Lines
of Works in Opera Omnia

Reference is made to catalogue numbers, followed by Opera
Omnia VOLUME/page in parenthesis. Titles of works are in
capital letters; first lines of arias and ensembles in lower case;
probable composers are set off with oblique lines.

Abbassa l'orgoglio, o spirito superbo, 63d (IV:18)
Ad annientarmi potea discendere, 141z (XII:130)
ADDIO L', 110 (X:10)
ADORO TE DEVOTE, 56 (XVII/1:1)
ADRIANO IN SIRIA, 140 (XIV:1)
A fondar le mie grandezze, 63f (IV:25)
AGNUS DEI, 39, 40 (XXIII:162, 160)
AH, CHE SENTO IN MEZZO AL CORE, 84 (XXII:93)
Ahi che pena, 147f (III:29)
Ah, ingrato, m'inganni, 140k (XIV:80)
AH! MI DIVIDON L'ANIMA, GLI ACERBI AFFANI MIEI, 123 (XIX:1)
Ah perfida! E poi trattarmi così, 139g (XI/2:33)
AH SE SOFFERSI, O DIO!, 81 (XXII:27)
/Alberti, Domenico/, 7 (XXI:7)
Al grande onore saro innalzato, 144y (II:107)
Alla vita, al portamento, 139b (XI/2:1)
Al real piede ognora, 146c (IX:11)
A lui donai l'mio core, 141L (XII:56)
AMERÒ FINCHÈ IL MIO CORE, 85 (XXII:35)
Amor che si sta accolto, 141n (XII:71)
AMOR FEDELE, 111 (X:20)
Andrò ramingo e solo, 146j (IX:49)
Appena spira l'aura soave, 64e (I:17)
Apportator son io, 145k (XXIV:73)
/Aresti, Floriano/, 101 (XXII:39)
A Serpina penserete, 137f (XI/1:36)
A sfogar lo sdegno mio, 63q (IV:88)
Aspettare e non venire, 137b (XI/1:36)
/Auletta, Pietro/, 148 (XXV)
A una povera polacca, 138b (XI/3:5)
A un lampo di timore, 146e (IX:20)
A un semplice istante, 140h (XIV:56)
AVE VERUM, 57 (XVII/1:12)
Avventurose spose, 144f (II:17)

BASTA, COSÌ TI INTENDO, 124 (XIX:1)
BEATUS VIR QUI TIMET, 72 (VIII:213)
Bella mia, se ton tuo sposo, 148e (XXV:14)
Belle e cocenti lacrime, 139f (XI/2:28)
Benche sia forte il cor, 146v (IX:138)
BENDATO PARGOLETTO, 86 (XXII:59)
/Bononcini, Antonio/, 90, 99, 104, 108 (XXI:24, 30, 63, 55)

Cacciatemi, cacciatemi, 141v (XII:113)
Cadrò contento dal duolo oppresso, 117d (X:33)
CANTO DEL PASTORE, IL, 112 (X:44)
Cara Dorina, ascolta, 147j (III:49)
CARA, TU RIDI, 87 (XXII:65)
Caro, perdonami, 138g (XI/3:38)
Caro, son tua così, 145u (XXIV:153)
Che fiero martire, 143d (XX:16)
Che non mi disse un dì, 145m (XXIV:82)
/Chiarini, Pietro/, 147 (III:5)
Chi disse che la femmina, 144r (II:69)
Chi fa bene?, 63L (IV:62)
Chi ha il cor fra la catene, 141aa (XII:134)
Chi mi sgrida?, 143p (XX:94)
CHI NON CREDE ALLE MEI PAROLE, 88 (XXII:86)
Chi non ode e chi non vede, 117a (X:33)
/Chinzer, Giovanni/, 123 (XIX:1)
Ch'io muti consiglio, 63b (IV:10)
Chi soffre senza pianto, 140g (XIV:47)
/Ciampi, Vincenzo Legrenzio, 106 (XXII:66)
Cieco che non vid'io, 63i (IV:42)
Ci troveremo gnorsì, gnorsì, 144ee (II:131)
Clori, se mai rivolgi, 112a (X:44)
Come chi gioca alle palle, 148g (XXV:22)
CONCERTINO, FOUR VIOLINS, VIOLA, CELLO AND CONTINUO, 26, 27, 28,
     29, 30, 31 (VII:1-83)
CONCERTO A CINQUE, 32 (XXI:95)
CONCERTO, FLUTE AND STRINGS, 33, 34 (XXI:71-86)
Con eco giuliva risponda ogni riva, 143x (XX:148)
CONFITEBOR TIBI, DOMINE, 66 (VIII:170)
CONFUSA, SMARRITA, 125 (XIX:34)
Con questa paroline, 141c (XII:13)
CONTADINA ASTUTA LA, 139 (XI/2:1)
Contento forse vivere, 110c (X:10)
Contento forse vivere, 140s (XIV:128)
Contento tu sarai, 137h (XI/1:51)
CONTRASTI CRUDELI, 113 (X:57)
COR PRIGIONIERO, 118 (XXII:70)
Cor prigioniero che, vaneggiando, 118a (XXII:70)

Così dunque si teme, 63h (IV:33)
CREDO, 38 (XIX:supp)
CREDO, 41 (XXIII:139)

Dal labbro che ti accende, 140b (XIV:10)
Dalsigre, ahi mia Dalsigre!, 114a (X:1)
D'amor l'arcano ascoso, 141d (XII:19)
D'amor la saetta già svelsi dal core, 146g (IX:30)
Da rio funesto turbine, 141s (XII:94)
Deh fate piano, piano, 144x (II:100)
DEH, T'ACCHETA E NON NEGARMI, 126 (XIX:71)
Deh volgi i vaghi rai all'alma, 112c (X:44)
Del destin non vi lagnate, 145f (XXIV:36)
Del fiero tuo dolore, 141r (XII:90)
Del mio valore al lampo, 141m (XX:69)
/Di Capua, Rinaldo/, 124 (XIX:38)
Di così dolce speme, 141i (XII:44)
DIES IRAE, 80 (XXVI:47)
Digli ch'è un infedele, 140r (XIV:124)
Dio s'offende, 63c (IV:13)
Dite ch'ogni momento, 114b (X:1)
DIXIT DOMINUS, 67, 68, 73 (VIII:1-113)
Dolce auretta ch'alletta, 64j (I:41)
DOMINE AD ADIUVANDUM, 51 (XVII/I:15)
Dopo il periglio de la tempesta, 142r (XX:107)
DORME, BENIGNE JESU, 58 (XVII/1:29)
Dove mai raminga vai?, 63g (IV:29)
Dove vado, dove sono, 144bb (II;122)
/Durante, Francesco/, 58, 59 (XVII/1:29, 66)

Ecco il giorno più felice, 147h (III:38)
Ecco il povero Tracollo, 138d (XI/3:18)
Ecco, Tirsi, quel mirto, 113b (X:57)
E'dover che le luci, 63p (IV:82)
Egli è di questo petto, 144cc (II:124)
EMPIO AMOR. AMOR TIRANNO, 89 (XXII:1)
È PU VER, 90 (XXII:24)
E'strano il mio tormento, 144h (II:25)
Euridice e dove sei?, 115b (X:82)

Fiamma ignota nell'alma mi scende, 145w (XXIV:168)
FLAMINIO, 141 (XII:1)
Fra fronda e fronda, 63n (IV:70)

Fra gli scogli e la procella, 148b (XXV:4)
Fra poco assiso in trono, 140t (XIV:139)
Fra tanti affani miei, 143e (XX:20)
FRATE 'NNAMARATO LO, 144 (II:1)

/Gallo, Domenico/, 12,13,14,15,16,17,18,19,20,21,22,23 (V:1-128)
/Galuppi, Baldassare/, 88, 147a (XXII: 86, III:5)
GELOSO SCHERNITO IL, 147 (III:5)
Gemo in un punto e fremo, 145s (XXIV:134)
Già che vi piace, o Dei, 146q (IX:104)
Già in te rinascere, 64k (I:45)
/Giay, Giovanni Antonio/, 134 (XIX:67)
Gioa mia, mi vuoi lasciare, 144q (II:64)
Giusti numi che scorgete, 143i (XX:43)
Gnora, credetemi, 144L (II:41)
Grandi, è ver son le tue pene, 145L (XXIV:76)
GUGLIEMO D'AQUITANIA, 63 (IV:1)

/Hasse, Johann Adolph/, 139 (XI/2:1-37)
Ha un giusto da stordire, 148c (XXV:6)

IL CANTO DEL PASTORE, 112 (X:44)
IL GELOSO SCHERNITO, 147 (III:5)
IL MAESTRO DI MUSICA, 142, 148 (XXV:1)
Il nocchier ne la tempesta, 146s (IX:114)
IL PRIGIONIERO SUPERBO, 143 (XX:1)
Il signor vuol ch'ha me solo, 64i (I:36)
Il tormento ch'ha sto core, 142n (II:53)
IMMAGINI DOLENTI PERCHÉ NEL COR TI STANNO?, 127 (XIX:5)
INCARNATUS, 42 (XXIII:156)
IN COELESTIBUS REGNIS, 52 (XVII/1:34)
INGRATO NON SARÒ, 91 (XXII:61)
IN HAC DIE, 53 (XVII/1:38)
In mar turbato e nero, 146bb (IX:168)
In mezzo a questo petto, 141p (XII:81)
Innalziam lodi al signori, 64b (I:5)
In queste spiaggie amene, 114a (X:20)
In singolar tenzone, 144ii (II:147)
In te ripone il cor, 64g (I:26)
Invocando il doce nome, 64r (I:75)
IO NON SO DOVE MI STO, 92 (XXII:88)
Io son d'un animuccio, 141q (XII:85)
Io ti dissi e a dirti torno, 144hh (II:140)

Io ti vorrei pietosa, 112b (X:44)
Ite a godere ch'io non v'invidio, 141dd (XII:153)

LA CONTADINA ASTUTA, 139 (XI/2:1)
L'ADDIO, 110 (X:10)
LAETATUS SUM, 69 (VIII:274)
LA MORTE DI S. GIUSEPPE, 64 (I:1)
/Lampugnani, Giovanni Battista/, 98, 103 (XXII:10, 15)
L'ardor che cresce in seno, 64p (I:68)
Lascia d'offendere, 63r (IV:92)
La sciorte mia è accussì barbara, 141o (XII:77)
LA SERVA PADRONA, 137 (XI/1:1)
LAUDATE PUERI DOMINUM, 65, 74 (VIII:234)
Le dirà che il suo vago cicisbeo, 144e (II:13)
/Leo, Leonardo/, 73, 92 (VIII:113-169, XXII:88)
Leon piagato a morte, 140p (XIV:109)
L'esser geloso e misero, 147i (III:43)
L'estremo pegno almeno, 140v (XIV:148)
Le virtuose che son famose, 148h (XXV:28)
Lieto così talvolta, 140j (XIV:68)
L'infelice in questo stato, 145t (XXIV:147)
LIVIETTA E TRACOLLO, 138 (XI/3:1)
Lo conosco a quegli occhietti, 137e (XI/1:24)
LO FRATE 'NNAMARATO, 144 (II:1)
L'oggetto del cor mio, 141y (XII:127)
L'OLIMPIADE, 145 (XXIV:1)
LONTANANZA, 114 (X:1)
Luce degli occhi miei, 110a (X:10)

MAESTRO DI MUSICA IL, 142, 148 (XXV:1)
MAGNIFICAT, 59 (VII/1:66)
Marito mio bello, 147e (III:20)
MASS, C MAJOR, 48 (XXIII:1)
MASS, D MAJOR, 46 (XV/2:1)
MASS, D MAJOR, 49 (XXIII:64)
MASS, F MAJOR, 45 (XVIII:2)
MASS, F MAJOR, 47 (VI:2)
Mentre dormir amor fomenti, 145i (XXIV:52)
Mentre l'erbetta pasce l'agnella, 141b (XII:5)
Menzogniero, mancatore!, 113d (X:57)
M'intendeste? non pavento, 143g (XX:31)
Mio caro signor Maestro, 148m (XXV:57)
Mi palpita il core, 144w (II:96)
MISERERE MEI, 70, 71 (XIII:1-77)
Miseri affetti miei, 117c (X:33)

MISERO ME, QUAL GELIDO TORMENTO, 128 (XIX:42)
MO CHE TE STREGNO, 119 (XIX:supp)
Morta tu mi vuoi vedere, 144j (II:34)
MORTE DI S. GIUSEPPE LA, 64 (I:1)
Mostro crudele, orrendo, 146cc (IX:178)
Muoiono le fenici, 64d (I:14)

Nei giorni tuoi felici, 145j (XXIV:63)
Nel chiuso centro, 115a (X:82)
Nella fatal mia sorte, 145y (XXIV:183)
Nel rimirar quei luoghi, 111b (X:20)
No, la speranza, 145r (XXIV:122)
Non abbia più riposo, 141bb (XII:139)
Non c'e conguaglio sul qual tu conti, 144gg (II:137)
Non gemiti o lamenti udrai, 113g (X:71)
NON MI TRADIR, 93 (XXII:43)
Non mi vedete voi, 144d (II:9)
Non potrà sopra il mio core, 116d (XXII:75)
Non si cchella ch'io lassaje, 141g (XII:37)
Non si muove, non rifiata, 137h (XI/3:41)
NON SO DONDE VIENE, 129 (XIX:51)
Non so donde viene, 145z (XXIV:187)
Non sperare dai fieri incanti, 118b (XXII:70)
NON TI MINACCHIO SDEGNE, 130 (XIX:29)
Non vò tal sposo, 141h (XII:42)
Non vo'più dargli ascolto, 142b (XXV)

O buon pastor, 64n (I:58)
O care selve, 145e (XXIV:27)
O d'Euridice, n'andro festoso, 115c (X:82)
Odio di figlia altera l'ambizioso core, 146m (IX:70)
Ogni pena più spietata, 144k (II:36)
O che sproposito, che melensaggine, 148a (XXV:1)
Oh degli uomini Padre e degli Dei, 145aa (XXIV:194)
Oh Dio! sei troppo barbara, 141j (XII:48)
OLIMPIADE L', 145 (XXIV:1)
Ombre mute, oscuri orrori, 143q (XX:99)
Or che dal reglio trono, 146i (IX:44
ORFEO, 115 (X:82)
/Orlandini, Giuseppe Maria/, 131, 136 (XIX:62, 82)
Or risponder ti debbo, 113f (X:71)
O SACRUM CONVIVIUM, 60 (XVII/1:97)
Ove tu, ben mio, 110b (X:10)

Si lieto fine alla burletta, 147m (III:66)
Si Masacco, muori presto, 147L (III:61)
SINFONIA TO AN UNKNOWN OPERA, 35, 37 (XIX:X,I)
SISTE, SUPERBE FRAGOR, 61 (XVII/1:121)
Si stordisce il villanello, 144v (II:81)
Si, tiranna, fra dure ritorte, 146y (IX:155)
Si vedisse ccà dinto a sto core, 63e (IV:21)
Si, vorrei parlare, 144t (II:78)
Soave ferite, 64f (I:22)
SO CH'È FANCIULLO AMORE, 132 (XIX:47)
So ch'è fanciullo amore, 145o (XXIV:98)
S'oda, Augusto, fin sull'etra, 140w (XIV:158)
Sola mi lasci a piangere, 140i (XIV:65)
Soleva il traditor, 146h (IX:35)
So! mpazzuto, che m'è dato, 63o (IV:77)
SONATA, CELLO AND CONTINUO, 11 (XXI:46)
SONATA, HARPSICHORD, 1, 6, 7, 8, 9, 10 (XXI:1-16)
SONATA, ORGAN, 2 (XXI:41)
SONATA, VIOLIN AND STRINGS, 36 (XXI:54)
SONATA, TWO VIOLINS AND CONTINUO, 12, 13, 14, 15, 16, 17, 18, 19, 20,
    21, 22, 23, 24, 25 (V:1-128)
Son imbrogliato io già, 137q (XI/1:43)
Son moglie, non schiava, 147b (III:10)
Son qual per mare ignoto, 145x (XXIV:173)
Son timida fanciulla, 142a (XXV:67)
Son tutto in tempesta, 147d (III:17)
Splenda il sol di luce adorno, 143b (XX:6)
Splenda per voi sereno, 140m (XIV:91)
Splende fra noi seren di pace, 148k (XXV:39)
Sposo, và: verrà quel dì, 64o (I:64)
Sprezzo il furor del vento, 140c (XIV:15)
Sta barca desparata, 141x (XII:123)
STABAT MATER, 77 (XXVI:1)
Stizzoso, mio stizzoso, 137d (XI/1:17)
SUITE, HARPSICHORD, 3, 4, 5 (XXI:20-31)
Sul mio cor so ben qual sia, 140d (XIV:27)
Sul vago praticello, 139c (XI/2:4)
Suo caro e dolce amore, 144z (II:110)
Superbo di me stesso, 145b (XXIV:9)
SUPER FLUMINA BABYLONIS, 62 (XVII/2:1)
Su, su alle gioie, 144jj (II:150)

Talor del fiume placido, 146n (IX:78)
Talor guerriero invitto, 145c (XXIV:16)
TALOR SE IL VENTO FREME, 133 (XIX:55)
/Terradellas, Domenico/, 133, 135 (XIX:55, 22)
Ti perdi e confondi al nome di morte, 140u (XIV:143)

Viva il figlio, 145bb (XXIV:203)
Viva, viva il divo Augusto, 146b (IX:6)
Vo'dirti basso, basso, 148d (XXV:11)
Voglio dal tuo dolore, 146u (IX:134)
Vola al ciel, anima bella, 63t (IV:99)
Vola intorno al primo raggio, 64m (I:53)
Volgi a me le vaghe ciglia, 143u (XX:129)
Vorrei . . . oh Dio' ma vedo, 139e (XI/2:16)
VORREI POTER ALMENO, 109 (XXII:52)
Vuoi punir l'ingrato amante, 140f (XIV:43)
Vuoi un grido da me?, 147c (III:16)

APPENDIX
Attributed Works Omitted from Opera Omnia

Most of the compositions listed in this appendix exist in manuscripts or early printed editions; the others, although mentioned in the literature, have not been located. In all cases, the numbered references indicate monographs, articles and library catalogues listed in the bibliography. As stressed above, no attempt has been made to verify the information provided in the references.

The systematic arrangement parallels that of the Thematic Catalogue: works which may be presumed authentic are listed first, followed by doubtful (?) and then spurious (X) compositions. The enumeration begins with 200; the gaps in the numerical sequence, occurring at the end of each sub-category, were left to accommodate works yet to be uncovered.

Each entry includes the catalogue number, the title or textual incipit and (where known) the setting and/or key. As in the Plaine and Easie Code, an exclamation mark means an "incorrect" key signature (see p. xi above). Where the source is an early printed edition, place, publisher and date of publication (when known) are given in parentheses. When available, noteworthy information is set off with oblique lines; for example, variant spellings of Pergolesi's name, possible other composers, etc.

The right hand column indicates:

FIRST LINE: reference(s) cited (see bibliography).

SECOND LINE AND FOLLOWING LINES: where known, RISM abbreviations of libraries holding manuscripts or early printed editions of attributed works. A list of library abbreviations used in this catalogue appears on p. 91.

Instrumental Music

FOR SOLO INSTRUMENT

200.	Lesson, Harpsichord, no. 1, C major (London: Longman & Broderip, ca. 1780)	2, 3, 9 GB: Lbm
201.	Lesson, Harpsichord, no. 2, F major (London: Longman & Broderip, ca. 1780)	2, 3, 9 GB: Lbm
202.	Lesson, Harpsichord, no. 3, A minor (London: Longman & Broderip, ca. 1780)	2, 3, 9 GB: Lbm
203.	Lesson, Harpsichord, no. 4, G major (London: Longman & Broderip, ca. 1780)	2, 3, 9 GB: Lbm
204.	Lesson, Harpsichord, no. 5, D major (London: Longman & Broderip, ca. 1780)	2, 3, 9 GB: Lbm
205.	Lesson, Harpsichord, no. 8, C major[1] (London: Longman & Broderip, ca. 1780)	2, 3, 9 GB: Lbm
206.	Sonata, Harpsichord, no. 1, A major (London: Longman, Lukey & Co., ca. 1770)	2, 3, 4, 9, 14 GB: Lbm
207.	Sonata, Harpsichord, no. 3, G major[2] (London: Longman, Lukey & Co., ca. 1770)	2, 3, 4, 9, 14 GB: Lbm

---

[1]Of this collection of lessons (cat. nos. 200-205), entitled A Second Set of Eight Lessons for the Harpsichord, Lesson no. 6 is published in the Opera Omnia as Suite, Harpsichord, no. 2, E major (see our catalogue no. 4), while Lesson no. 7 appears in the Opera Omnia as Suite, Harpsichord, no. 1, E major (see our catalogue no. 3).

[2]Of this collection of sonatas (cat. nos. 206-212), entitled Eight Lessons for the Harpsichord, Sonata no. 2, appears in the Opera Omnia as Suite, Harpsichord, no. 3, D major (see our catalogue no. 5).

---

208.   Sonata, Harpsichord, no. 4, C minor!   2, 3, 4, 9, 14
        (London: Longman, Lukey & Co., ca. 1770)   GB:Lbm

209.   Sonata, Harpsichord, no. 5, G minor   2, 3, 4, 9, 14
        (London: Longman, Lukey & Co., ca. 1770)   GB:Lbm

210.   Sonata, Harpsichord, no. 6, C minor!   2, 3, 4, 9, 14
        (London: Longman, Lukey & Co., ca. 1770)   GB:Lbm

211.   Sonata, Harpsichord, no. 7, F major   2, 3, 4, 9, 14
        (London: Longman, Lukey & Co., ca. 1770)   GB:Lbm

212.   Sonata, Harpsichord, no. 8, D major   2, 3, 4, 9, 14
        (London: Longman, Lukey & Co., ca. 1770)   GB:Lbm

213. X Propter magnam, Organ   7
        (London: Vincent Novello, 1831)   GB:Lbm

FOR TWO TO FOUR INSTRUMENTS

230.   Sonata, 2 Violins and Bass, F major   25
        /Bergolese/   S:Uu

231.   Sonata, Violin and Bass, G major[3]   2, 9
                                                                      GB:Ckc

FOR FIVE OR MORE INSTRUMENTS

240.   Concerto, 2 Harpsichords and Strings, C major   2, 9
                                                                      US:AA

241.   Piccola Sinfonia, 2 Violins, Viola and Bass, Eb major   2, 9
                                                                      I:Rsc

242.   Simphonia, 2 Violins, Viola and Cello, Bb major   11
        /Pere Golese/   US:R

243.   Simphonia, 2 Violins, Viola and Cello, F major   11
        /Pere Golese/   US:R

244.   Simphonia, 2 Violins, Viola and Cello, G major   11
        /Pere Golese/

245. X Sinfonia, 2 Violins, Viola, 2 Clarini and Timpani,   3, 4
        C major

---

[3]A transposed arrangement of the second movement of this composition appears in the Opera Omnia as Sonata, Harpsichord, no. 1, A major (see our catalogue no. 1).

Sacred Vocal Music

FRAGMENTS OF MASSES

260.	Credo, 4 Voices and Orchestra, D minor	9, 26 F:Pn A:Wn
261.	Gloria in excelsis Deo, Voice and Orchestra	5 I:Nc GB:Lcm
262.	Sanctus, 4 Voices	3, 4
263. X	Benedictus (Paris: A. Lafitte, 1859)	7

MASSES

270.	Mass, 10 Voices, 2 Choruses, Orchestra and Organ, D major	3 I:Nc
271.	Mass, SATB and Continuo, D minor	5, 9, 23 GB:Lbm
272.	Mass, 2 Voices, Chorus and Orchestra, F major	2
273.	Mass, 4 Voices and Orchestra, F major	2
274.	Requiem, 4 Voices and Orchestra	9 F:Pn
275.	Requiem cum offertorio	2, 3, 4, 5, 9 D:OJ

MOTETS

285.	Aura sacratis amoris, S and Orchestra	1, 7, 9 B:Bsg
286.	Conturbat mentem, S and Orchestra	2, 3, 4, 5, 9 D:Bds D:W
287.	De placido torrente	2, 3, 4, 5, 7, 9 B:Bsg
288.	De profundus	1, 2
289.	Domine ad adiuvandum, SATB and Orchestra, D major	1, 9, 23 GB:Lcm GB:Lbm D:MÜs
290.	Ecce pietatis signa, S and Orchestra	9 I:Mc
291.	Ecce superbos Hostes, S and Orchestra	2, 7, 9 B:Bsg
292.	In campo armato pugno, S and Orchestra	5, 7 D:Bjg
293.	O salutaris hostia, TB and Continuo[4]	2, 4, 7, 9 GB:Lbm
294.	Peccator crudelis, 4 Voices, G minor	5, 7 I:Vnm
295.	Salus et Gloria, A and Orchestra[5]	3, 4, 5, 7 D:SW
296.	Salve Creator[6]	3, 4, 5, 7 D:W
297.	Salve Redemptor, A or Bar and Orchestra[6]	3, 4, 5, 7 D:KG

---

[4]A probable autograph,   1729; see Reference 9.

[5]Same as setting of Salve Regina; see Reference 3.

[6]German adaptation of Salve Regina; see Reference 3.

298.	Septem verba a Christo, 3 Voices and Orchestra	1, 4, 8, 28 CH: Zz
299.	Sequentia olim tempore - Missae septem dolorum	2, 3, 4, 5, 9 D: LUh
300.	Sol resplendet, with 2 Orchestras	2, 7, 9 GB: T
301.	Sumi benigne (Sei mir gnadig), 4 Voices (Stuttgart: J. C. Weeber, 1857)	3, 5
302.	Te ergo quaesimus, ST and Harpsichord	5 I: Rsc
303.	Tuba et tympano, S and Orchestra	2, 9 B: Bsg
304.	Utique resonando	2, 3, 4, 5, 7, 9 I: Nf
305.	Verbum Christi, 4 Voices and Orchestra	2, 3, 4, 5, 9 D: Mbs

ORATORIO AND SACRED DRAMA

325.	La nascita del Redentore	2, 3, 4, 7, 8, 9
326.	Il Pentimento	2, 8, 9, 22 GB: Lbm GB: Lcm
327.	? La Morte di Abel	2, 7, 8, 9, 28 CH: Zz
328.	X Oratorio della Passione	7
329.	X Planctus animo poenitensis ad Matrem dolorosam	7 GB: Lbm

PSALMS

| 335. | Dixit Dominus, SATB and Accompaniment, Bb major | 2, 9
D: MÜs |

84

336.	Dixit Dominus, SATB, Chorus, Strings, and Orchestra, D major	3, 4 D:Bds A:Wgm
337.	Laetatus sum, SSBB and Orchestra	3, 9 D:MÜs
338.	Laetatus sum, 5 Voices and Orchestra	3, 4, 5 I:Nc
339.	Laudate pueri Dominum, 5 Voices and Orchestra, A minor	5, 2, 9 A:Wgm
340.	Laudate pueri Dominum, 5 Voice Canon	2, 5 D:Bds
341.	Miserere mei, 9 Voices and Organ, A minor	2, 9 D:SW
342.	Miserere mei, 4 Voices and Orchestra, Bb major	2, 3, 4, 5, 9 D:KG
343.	Miserere mei, 4 Voices and Orchestra, C major	1
344.	Miserere mei, C minor	F:Pn
345.	Miserere mei, 9 Voices and Organ, D minor	2, 9 GB:Lbm
346.	Miserere mei, 4 Voices and Orchestra, F major	4, 5, 9 F:Pn
347.	Miserere mei, SATB and Orchestra, G minor	2, 4, 5, 9 F:Pn B:Bc GB:Lbm
348.	Quis sicut, B and Orchestra	2, 9 B:Br
349.	Sicut erat, 4 Voices and Orchestra, D major[7]	1, 2, 3, 4, 7, 9 I:Nc

[7]May be identical with Cum Sancto Spiritu of Mass in D for five voices; see References 7 and 9.

350. ⁶ X Deus misereator nostri   7

SACRED CANTATA

355.   La Maddalena al sepolcro, S and Accompaniment   19
                                                                   I:A

SEQUENCES AND ANTIPHONS

360.   Lauda Sion salvatorem   2, 5, 9
               (Turin, 1929)

361.   Salve Regina, S and Orchestra, F major[8]   2, 9
                                                                   I:Mc

First page, *O salutaris hostia.* (autograph?). London: British Museum. No. 293.

[8]Possibly a transposed version of Salve Regina in A minor; see Reference 2.

Secular Vocal Music

CHAMBER ARIAS

382.	Pellegrino ch'infolto orror	1
383.	Per fuggirti io peno avrò	3, 4
384.	Saggio nocchiero	21 B:Bc
385.	Tergi quel pianto, o cara	21 B:Bc
386.	Tra fronda e fronda	1
387.	Tremende oscure atroci	21 B:Bc
388.	Un caro e dolce sguardo	7
389.	Vado a morir ben mio	1

CHAMBER CANTATAS

400.	A te torna il tuo fileno, S and Strings	1, 3, 4, 8
401.	Della città vicina di Mergellina	2, 7, 9 D:MÜs
402.	Il tempo felice (scenic prelude)[9]	2, 3, 4, 7, 8
403.	Nigella, ah mia Nigella, Bb major	22 GB:Lbm
404.	Ove tu, ben mio non sei, S and Strings	1, 3, 4, 8
405.	Quest'è amor, quest'è fede	2, 7, 9 D:MÜs
406. X	L'aura, il ruscello, il fonte	7
407. X	Berenice che fai	7
408. X	Che farò, che	7

[9]The first part was probably composed by Pergolesi, the second part by L. Sabbatino; see References 2 and 8.

FRAGMENTS OF OPERAS

415.   La ragion, gli affetti   23
                                                         GB:Lbm

INTERMEZZI

420.   An untitled intermezzo with characters Nibbio and Nerina   8, 9

421. ? Amor fa l'uomo cieco (o "la sorte degli amanti")[10] 1, 2, 3, 4, 7, 8, 9, 15

422. X La Bohemia   6
                                                         F:Pc

423. X Dalina e Balbo   3, 4, 6, 8
                                                         D:DS

OPERAS

435. ? Recimero   1, 2, 3, 4, 7, 8

436. X Achille in Sciro /Domenico Sarri/   7

437. X Il Cavaliere Ergasto /Niccolò Piccinni/   3, 4, 7, 8
                                                         I:NO

438. X Il Temistocle   3, 4, 6, 7, 8, 20
                                                         I:BC

439. X Le Diable à Quatre   3, 4, 6, 8
                                                         F:Pc

440. X L'Orazio   7
           /Pietro Auletta/

441. X Lo Studente alla Moda   8
           /fragments from L'Olimpiade/

442. X Tracillo, Medico Ignorante   6
                                                         B:Bc
                                                         F:Pc

[10] This intermezzo was often performed with the opera "Salustia" which was composed by Pergolesi. It is probably a pastiche with arias by Chiarini, Pergolesi and Goldini; see Reference 15.

Miscellany

450.   Solfeggi, 2 and 3 Voices, in Three Parts,
        SA, SAB, AB[11]   1, 2, 3, 4, 7, 8
                                                  I:Nc

451.   Solfeggio, Harpsichord Accompaniment   2, 3, 4
                                                  I:Nc

452. ? Venerabilis barba cappuccinorum, TB
         (Scherzo fatto ai Cappuccini di Pozzuoli)[12]   1, 2, 4, 7, 8, 9, 23
                                                I:Mc
                                                I:Nc
                                            D:Mbs
                                            A:Wgm
                                          GB:Lbm

---

[11]This is a possible autograph; see Reference 4.

[12] The fact that this work is known under two different titles seems to have led some authorities to list it as two different works.

Library Abbreviations

A: AUSTRIA

Wgm   Vienna, Gesellschaft der Musikfreunde
Wn   Vienna, Österreichische Nationalbibliothek

B: BELGIUM

Bc   Brussels, Bibliothèque du Conservatoire royal de musique
Br   Brussels, Bibliothèque royale de Belgique
Bag   Brussels, Sainte-Gudule

CH: SWITZERLAND

Zz   Zürich, Zentralbibliothek (und Bibliothek der Allgemeinen
        Musikgesellschaft)

D: GERMANY

Bds   Berlin, Deutsche Staatsbibliothek
Bjg   Berlin, Joachimstalchen Gymnasium
DS   Darmstadt, Hessische Landes- und Hochschul-Bibliothek
KG   Königsberg, Bibliothek
LUh   Lübeck, Bibliothek der Hansestadt
Mbs   München, Bayerische Staatsbibliothek
MÜs   Münster, Santini-Bibliothek
OJ   Formerly the Otto Jahn Library
SW   Schwerin, Landesbibliothek
W   Wölfenbuttel, Herzog-August-Bibliothek

F: FRANCE

Pc   Paris, Bibliothèque du Conservatoire
Pn   Paris, Bibliothèque nationale

GB: GREAT BRITAIN

Ckc	Cambridge, King's College
Lbm	London, British Museum
Lcm	London, Royal College of Music
T	Tenbury, St. Michael's College

I: ITALY

A	Assisi, Biblioteca communale
Bc	Bologna, Biblioteca del Conservatorio (Liceo Musicale)
Mc	Milan, Biblioteca del Conservatorio
Nc	Naples, Biblioteca del Conservatorio
NF	Naples, Biblioteca Oratoriana dei Filippini (o Girolamini)
NO	Novara, Archivio del Duomo e Archivio di S. Gaudenzio
Rsc	Rome, Biblioteca S. Cecilia (Conservatorio)
Vnm	Venice, Biblioteca nazionale Marciana

S: SWEDEN

Uu	Uppsala, Universitetsbiblioteket

US: UNITED STATES

AA	Ann Arbor (Michigan), Clements Library and General Library, University of Michigan.
R	Rochester (New York), Sibley Music Library, Eastman School of Music.

INDEX TO APPENDIX
Works Omitted from Opera Omnia

Reference is made to item numbers in the Appendix. See also
Index to Thematic Catalogue for composers, titles, and
first lines of works in Opera Omnia.

BIBLIOGRAPHY
References Cited for Attribution

Books

1   Faustini-Fasini, E. "Elenco completo delle opere di G. B. Pergolesi."
    G. B. Pergolesi (Milan, 1900) 90-94.

2   Margadonna, Michele. "Elenco delle opere di G. B. Pergolesi."
    Pergolesi (Milan, 1961) 199-204.

3   Radiciotti, Giuseppe. "Le Opere di G. B. Pergolesi." Pergolesi
    (Milan, 1935) 175-200.

4   Radiciotti, Giuseppe. "Verzeichnis der Werke Pergolesis."
    Giovanni Battista Pergolesi Leben und Werke, ed. Antoine
    E. Cherbuliez (Zurich/Stuttgart, 1954) 411-22.

5   Zanetti, Emilia. "Contributo a una Bibliografia della Musica Sacra
    di G. B. Pergolesi." G. B. Pergolesi note e documenti raccolti
    in occasione della settimana celebrativa (Siena, 1942) 89-100.

Encyclopedia Entries

6   Eitner, Robert. Biographisch-bibliographisches Quellen-Lexicon
    der Musiker und Musikgelehrten der christlichen Zeitrechnung
    bis zur Mitte der 19. Jahrhunderts (Leipzig, 1904) VII, 370-71.

7   Hucke, Helmut. "Pergolesi." Die Musik in Geschichte und
    Gegenwart, ed. Friedrich Blume (Kassel/Basel, 1962) X,
    1047-63.

8   Long, Marguerite. "Pergolèse." Encyclopédie de la Musique,
    ed. Francois Michel et al. (Paris, 1961) III, 408-11.

9   Walker, Frank. "Pergolesi: Catalogue of Works." Grove's
    Dictionary of Music and Musicians, ed. Eric Blom, 5th ed.
    (London, 1954) VI, 632-33.

Periodical Articles

10 Brook, Barry S. "The Simplified Plaine and Easie Code System for Notating Music: A Proposal for International Adoption." Fontes Artis Musicae, XII/2-3 (1965) 156-60.

11 Clayton, Humphrey. "Three String Quartets Attributed to Pergolesi." Music and Letters, XIX (1938) 453-59.

12 Cudworth, Charles L. "Notes on the Instrumental Works Attributed to Pergolesi." Music and Letters, XXX/4 (1949) 321-28.

13 Cudworth, Charles L. "Ye Olde Spuriosity Shoppe." Notes, XII/1 (1954) 25-40; XII/4 (1955) 540-41.

14 Saint-Foix, Georges de. "Les maîtres de l'opéra bouffe dans la musique de chambre, à Londres." Rivista Musicale Italiana, XXXI/4 (1924) 507-26.

15 Walker, Frank. "Goldoni and Pergolesi." Monthly Musical Record, LXXX (October, 1950) 200-05.

16 Walker, Frank. "Pergolesiana." Music and Letters, XXXII/3 (1951) 295-96.

17 Walker, Frank. "Tre Giorni son che Nina: An Old Controversy Reopened." Musical Times, XC (December 1949) 432-35.

18 Walker, Frank. "Two Centuries of Pergolesi Forgeries and Misattributions." Music and Letters, XXX/4 (1949) 297-321.

Library Catalogues

19 Assisi. Catalogo del fondo musicale nella Biblioteca Comunale di Assisi. ed. Claudio Sartori (Milan, 1962) 319.

20 Bologna. Catalogo della biblioteca del Liceo musicale di Bologna G.B. Martini. ed. Gaetano Gaspari (Bologna, 1961) III, 329.

21 Brussels. Catalogue de la bibliothèque du Conservatoire Royal de Musique. ed. A. Wotquenne (Brussels, 1898-1912) II, 203, 219, 220.

22 London. Catalogue of the King's Music Library. ed. Hilda Andrews (London, 1929) II, 157-59.

23   London. Catalogue of manuscript music in the British Museum.
      ed. A. Hughes-Hughes (London, 1906-1909) I, 237, 305; II, 91,
      289, 300, 335.

24   London. Catalogue of printed books in the British Museum:
      Music in the Hirsch Library (London, 1959) 336.

25   Uppsala. Catalogue of the Gimo Collection of Italian manuscript
      music in the University Library of Uppsala. ed. Åke Davidsson
      (Uppsala, 1963) 69.

26   Vienna. Tabulae codicum manuscriptorum praeter Graecos et
      Orientales in Bibliotheca Palatina Vindobonensi Asservatorum.
      ed. C. Geroldi (Vienna, 1897) 304.

27   Washington. U.S. Library of Congress catalogue of orchestral
      music. ed. O.G.T. Sonneck (Washington, 1912) 333.

28   Zürich. Katalog der gedruckten und handschriftlichen Musikalien
      des 17. bis 19. Jahrhunderts im Besitze der Allgemeine Musik-
      gesellschaft Zürich. ed. Georg Walter (Zürich, 1960) 101.

Further References on
Authenticity and Attribution

Cudworth, Charles L. "Book Review: Vincent Duckles, Minnie Elmer and Pierluigi Petrobelli, Thematic Catalog of a Manuscript Collection of Eighteenth-Century Italian Instrumental Music in the University of California, Berkeley, Music Library." The Galpin Society Journal, XVIII (March, 1965) 140-41.

Cudworth, Charles L. "Pergolesi, Ricciotti and the Count of Bentinck." Kongress-Bericht der Internationale Gesellschaft fur Musikwissenschaft, Fifth Congress (Utrecht, 1952) 127-31.

Degrada, Francesco. "Alcuni falsi autografi pergolesiani." Rivista Italiana di Musicologia, I/1 (1966) 32-48.

Degrada, Francesco. "Falsi pergolesiani, Dagli apocrifi ai ritratti." Il Convegno Musicale, I (1964) 133-42.

Degrada, Francesco. "Le Messe di Giovanni Battista Pergolesi. Problemi di cronologia e d'attribuzione." Analecta Musicologica: Studien zur italienisch-deutschen Musikgeschichte, III (1966) 65-79.

Degrada, Francesco. "Uno sconosciuto intermezzo di Giovanni Battista Pergolesi." Studi di musicologia in onore di Guglielmo Barblan in occasione del LX compleanno (Florence, 1966) 79-91.

Duckles, Vincent, Minnie Elmer and Pierluigi Petrobelli. Thematic Catalog of a Manuscript Collection of Eighteenth-Century Italian Instrumental Music in the University of California, Berkeley (Berkeley and Los Angeles, 1963) 102-3.

Dunning, Albert. "Zur Frage der Autorschaft der Ricciotti und Pergolesi zugeschrieben Concerti Armonici." Oesterreichische Akademie der Wissenschaften, Anzeigen der Phil-Hist. Klasse, V (1963) 113-29.

Hell, Helmut. Die neopolitanische Opernsinfonie in der ersten Hälfte des 18. Jahrhunderts (Tutzing, 1971) 453-57.